BOUND ON EARTH

Jessica,

Your friendship and support mean so much.

Thank you! Love,

Angela Hallstrom

BOUND

ON
EARTH

A NOVEL

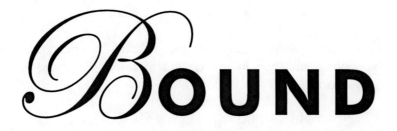

ANGELA
HALLSTROM

ISBN 978-0-9614960-9-8 (trade paper)

"Trying," *Irreantum*, Autumn 2003; 2nd Place *Irreantum* fiction contest

"Thanksgiving," *Dialogue* Vol. 38 no. 1, Spring 2005; winner of *Dialogue's* New Voices Award; *Dialogue's* "Best of the Year Award: Fiction;" and 2nd Place in the Utah Arts Council 48th Annual Writing Competition, Short Story Category, 2006.

"Christina" (previously titled "Unbroken"), *Irreantum* Vol. 7, No. 1 (2005)

"Accusation," *Dialogue* Vol. 40, No. 3, Fall 2007

"Who Do You Think You Are?" 1st Place *Salt Flats Annual* Emerging Writer Fiction Contest, 2007

Bound on Earth (previously titled *True and Faithful*), honorable mention, Utah Arts Council 48th Annual Writing Competition, Novel Category

Cover art by Anthony Sweat

PARABLES

PO Box 58
Woodsboro, MD 21798
www.parablespub.com

ACKNOWLEDGMENTS

I offer my thanks to the journals who published some of the stories in this book: "Thanksgiving" and "Accusation" in *Dialogue*; "Christina" (previously titled "Unbroken") and "Trying" in *Irreantum*; and "Who Do You Think You Are?" in *Salt Flats Annual*.

I would like to express my gratitude to the faculty of the Graduate Liberal Studies department at Hamline University, and Sheila O'Connor in particular. Without your wise guidance, this book would not exist. I also owe many thanks to the Association for Mormon Letters. My AML friends have inspired me, encouraged me, and worn down the path for me to follow. I am grateful, as well, to Anthony Sweat for his beautiful cover art, and to Elizabeth Petty Bentley for her careful and skillful editing.

I thank my extended family for their kindness, their example, and the love and faith they taught me all my life that (I hope) has found its way into this book. To my children Ethan, Elise, Jonas, and Wyatt: You are it. You are all.

And Forrest. A long time ago, you introduced me to a story about a little prince and a rose and the responsibility of love. Thank you for that—and for everything else.

"People have forgotten this truth," the fox said. "But you mustn't forget it. You become responsible forever for what you've tamed. You're responsible for your rose . . ."

"I'm responsible for my rose . . . ," the little prince repeated, in order to remember.

–ANTOINE DE SAINT-EXUPÉRY
The Little Prince

THE PALMERS

Joel Russell Palmer (b. 30 Mar 1920 Tropic, UT)
> sp: Tessa Louise Shaw (b. 9 July 1925 Logan, UT; m. 10 Feb 1946)

|

Nathan Joel Palmer (b. 14 Jan 1950 Salt Lake City, UT)
> sp: Alicia Rose Bennigan (b. 8 Sep 1950 Sandy, UT; m. 17 Jan 1972)

|

Marnie Lynne Palmer (b. 29 Mar 1974 Salt Lake City, UT)
> sp: Michael Roy Iverson (b. 19 Oct 1973 Minneapolis, MN; m. 7 Aug 1998)

|

Christina Joy Palmer (b. 12 Nov 1975 Salt Lake City, UT)
> sp: Curtis Leonard Gubler (b. 11 May 1975 Magna, UT; m. 26 Jun 1997)
> sp: James Anthony Moretti (b. 3 Nov 1976 Albuquerque, New Mexico; m. 1 Nov 2004)

|

Elizabeth Rose Palmer (b. 5 May 1981 Salt Lake City, UT)
> sp: Kyle Andrew Hewitt (b. 12 Jun 1981 Los Angeles, CA; m. 10 Dec 2002)

CONTENTS

2005

&

THANKSGIVING

BETH: LISTENING

"Take care," says my Grandma Tess. She is the first one to leave after Thanksgiving dinner because she can't drive at night. She has two hours' driving to do, north to Uncle Russell's house in Logan. She's worried about me. She wonders how I will bear up. She covers my hands with her own, and her skin is paper dry.

"Things seem hard right now, but you'll see your way through. You're my Beth. You've always been a strong one," she tells me.

I'm lucky to have a grandmother like her. I don't get the feeling she's lying to me. I don't get the feeling she's telling me only what I want to hear.

We stand by the open door and sunlight streams through her thinning hair.

"I'm hanging in there," I tell her. "Really, I am."

"You can do this," she says. "Yes, yes. You can."

Today, no one has said Kyle's name out loud. During dinner Aunt Christy said, "Do you think he's well enough to be trusted around the baby?" Everybody knew who "he" was. But I didn't look up from my turkey.

Finally my mom said, "Who knows, Christy," in that great tone she gets when the subject's about to be changed.

No one has said his name, but in his absence he seems just as powerfully present as he always has been. Everyone feels it. My sisters keep sliding the conversation around, trying to avoid topics like love and marriage, mental health and single motherhood. My dad keeps coming up behind me and putting his hands on my shoulders. Really, they may as well all just be saying, "Kyle, Kyle, Kyle." A big family chant.

I keep listening for the door. I told him not to come. I said, "Kyle, it's for the best. You know how my mom gets—it's nothing personal, she just wants some peace—but you can spend time with your own mom. You can see Stella tomorrow. You can see me tomorrow. We'll talk then, I promise, we will, but today is not the day. Today is not the day."

He yelled at me. "Heartless," he called me. "Homewrecker."

I said, "Kyle, you are not yourself. Can't you see that you are not yourself?"

KYLE: OUTSIDE

Kyle imagines the family inside the house, laughing, eating, Beth and her sisters teasing each other and telling their inside jokes. His father-in-law, Nathan, in his chair at the head of the table, his mother-in-law, Alicia, sitting just barely on the edge of her seat, tense as a cat, ready to jump up and get somebody butter or salt or more ice. All of them pretending they don't miss him, that he never existed, that they're better off now without him.

He knows the food they've been eating because he's had Thanksgiving at this house practically every year for the last eight years and it's always the same food, yams with the marshmallows on top, homemade stuffing with cranberries and pecans. Kyle always got a drumstick. He got one and Nathan got the other, because they were both dark-meat men. "A real man likes the dark stuff," Nathan would say, and it made Kyle happy, knowing that his wife's father thought of him as a real man. From the moment he first met the Palmers he's been trying hard, doing his best to be the kind of man he should be. He'd be lying if he said all the effort to seem cheerful and focused and strong hadn't worn him down a little, but he'd been willing to do it for her. For them. For all of them, the whole family. And what good has it done him? All they do is listen to Beth and her side of the story, her little tales she tells: Kyle did this, Kyle did that, like she's Little Miss Innocent, like nothing's her fault.

And now she gets to sit there at the table as if she never did anything wrong and he's left alone, parked in his car two blocks from their house, abandoned on Thanksgiving by the family that said he belonged to them, the family that acted so charitable and kind but really they were just waiting for him to slip up. Waiting for a mistake so they could pull out the rug and watch him rattle to the floor and say, See, you never were good enough for us, we never asked for you, we measured you and found you wanting.

Like at Stella's baby blessing last month, his own daughter's baby blessing, he comes and wants to be a part, that's all, but everybody's so hung up about his clothes, how they're not appropriate for church, but what do they expect when his own wife leaves him, abandons him to fend for himself in their little apartment, and he has nothing, no money, no love. Who wouldn't show up in shorts and a T-shirt if not just to make a statement, so they could see what they've reduced him to? And then when he goes up to the podium to speak and keeps talking, pouring out his heart about his sweet little daughter and his wife who has left him, and her family which has betrayed him, the bishop takes him by the elbow in the middle of it all to lead him away from the microphone and he looks down and there's Beth, sobbing, crying, holding his beautiful little daughter

3

wearing her beautiful white blessing dress, and he's thinking, what does she have to cry about? Why is she the one crying when she's kept everything for herself and left her own husband with nothing?

She keeps telling him, "Just get back on your medication and then we'll talk." Get back on your medication and then, maybe, then, someday, then, then, then, but he tells her they're poisoning him with it, he can feel it in his blood, eating at his cells, chewing little holes in his molecules to let the poison inside. Sometimes he thinks she's in on it—Beth, her family, the doctors, all of them, plotting together to poison him with those innocent-looking pills. He's even said to her, "Are you trying to kill me?" That's what he said the night she left him. "Are you trying to kill me?" All she could do was say, "Kyle, please, Kyle, please," the baby carrier hooked over her arm, Stella crying inside—and her father, Nathan, waiting for her in the car on the street so he could carry her away.

But they can't get rid of him as easy as that. He's earned his place. He has a right. They were there at the temple, they can't have forgotten when he was bound to their daughter—and so, yes, to them, to all of them—eternally. Meaning: Forever. Meaning: Without end. They're hoping he won't show up, of course, hoping he just burns himself out and disappears like a curl of smoke up into the sky. But he is a father, a husband, a member of this family. They cannot cut him off like a dead branch on a tree and leave him out in the street. And he will show them. He will behave. He has ironed his clothes and brought flowers for his mother-in-law and he's planned what he'll say to Beth—"You look beautiful, as always"—and then they will see that they shouldn't be afraid of him.

BETH: UNCOUPLED

My older sister Marnie and I are putting up Thanksgiving leftovers. We're in our parents' kitchen and all three of her boys race past us screaming.

"These kids are running circles around me," she says. She's not being metaphorical. Her boys are screaming good-natured screams —screams of joy, you might call them. But still.

I am putting up the pies. I take slices from each leftover pie and squeeze them together into one tin, pumpkin and French silk and lemon meringue side-by-side.

"They should sell pies this way," I say. "It makes more sense. The variety. People would snap them up."

"Well there you go," Marnie says. "Your million-dollar idea."

"I've been saved!" I say, and she laughs. I haven't told her about my money mess—well, Kyle's money mess, but since he's my husband, it's mine too—but I know that she knows. My mom's a talker and my sisters are worse. Secrets are hard to keep. For example, I know that Marnie's husband Mike makes $94,000 a year in his job as some kind of finance guy for General Mills. When Marnie heard I'd left Kyle, she was nice enough to call me up and ask if I wanted to come stay with her in Minnesota for a while—"Get away from it all," she said—but I told her no. First of all, I'd feel in the way. Second, I don't know if I could stand it, really, living with their cute little family in their brand new house, watching Mike swinging in the door from work at the end of the day and Marnie kissing him on the cheek. At least that's the way I imagine life goes at Marnie's house, and I don't know how much of it I could take.

Marnie points a spoon at my baby, Stella. "I don't think that child has made a peep in twenty minutes," she says. She pats her pregnant stomach with her free hand and smiles. "I put in an order for one like that this time. Hope God remembers."

Stella sits propped in the crook of the couch, gumming on a board book. She's a good baby, wide-eyed and calm. A lap-sitter, Marnie calls her. She's six months old and has yet to roll over back to front, but they tell me not to worry, so I don't.

"The mysteries of genetics," I say, and Marnie knows what I mean. Take Marnie and Mike—obedient, even-tempered types, both of them—and all three of their boys started screaming as soon as

5

they left the womb and haven't stopped since. And then you have me and Kyle. You'd think we'd be in for it, but we end up with this sweet baby girl, as even-keeled as they come. She's been sleeping through the night since she was four weeks old.

"You deserve your Stella," Marnie says. "She's lucky to have you."

Of course she's not, I want to say. Don't be ridiculous.

"See?" Marnie says, and I look where she's looking, at Stella's round face. "See how she watches you, wherever you go? She can't take her eyes off you."

I know, I know. Children see everything.

"Open your eyes and look at me," he'd say when we fought. He wouldn't let me turn around, walk away, glance at the floor or the sky. The last time we fought, before I left him, he grabbed me by the shoulders, tight. Shook me a little. "Look at me!" And I did: his green eyes lit with fury, his skin tight across his cheeks. Even then, a handsome man.

We are almost finished with the silver. Marnie stands at the sink with her arms in the hot soapy water and I stand beside her, rinsing and drying.

Mike comes up behind Marnie and smoothes his hands over her round belly. "Nap time?" he says into her ear.

Upstairs, their boys are thumping and jumping. I keep listening for howls of pain.

"Ha," Marnie says. "Right."

"I think Grandpa's been looking pretty anxious to go to the park, don't you? Give me five minutes and we'll have ourselves some quiet."

He leans down and I hear it as he kisses her on the neck. I pretend to disappear.

I am in a house of couples: halves of wholes, yins and yangs, eternal pairings. Marnie and Mike are here today. Tina and Jimmy. Aunt Christy and Uncle Rob. Everybody's touching each other, even my mom and dad. Alicia and Nathan. I've heard it so many times it's almost one name, Aleeshyanathan, like something you'd call an Indian princess. They seem to be touching a lot lately. I swear they hardly touched at all when I was a kid, or at least I didn't notice it, but now I see them all the time. Like now: his hand resting lightly against her back, her head tilted against his arm.

I'm lucky I have Stella to hold on to. My Aunt Christy keeps telling me, "Why don't you put that child down?" She says I just might spoil her. But I need her weight on my hip, her skin on my skin. She is mine and I am hers. Her heaviness keeps me pinned to the earth.

A few weeks ago my mom caught me crying in the bathroom. "You'll feel better in time," she told me. "You've made the right decision. A hard one, but the right one. You deserve to live your own life. You and Stella, together—you can make a good life."

I didn't answer her back. I just nodded like I agreed with her, mainly so she wouldn't worry. She thinks I should divorce him. She hasn't said it in so many words, but I can tell that's what she wants me to do. I can't talk about it, myself. Don't even like to think about it.

But I have abandoned him. My husband for eternity, and I've left him to himself. There are times I think I'm a terrible person. My mother tells me, "There's only so much you can do." She says, "You've got to think about your daughter." And I do. Constantly, constantly. I think of Kyle and I think of my daughter and I think of myself. I stay up half the night in my old twin bed at my parents' house listening to Stella breathing and sighing in her crib, and I wonder if I've ever made a good choice in my life.

So this is what I tell myself. Kyle and I—our story—it's like this news report I remember from last winter about a skier who got lost in the mountains. For days, the whole community was looking for him. They had search teams, helicopters, police dogs. But then a big storm came and blanketed any clues they might have found with a fresh layer of snow. The temperature dropped. They held a press conference and said, "We're calling off the search; we'll have to wait for springtime, for the thaw." The lost skier's father stood up in front of the cameras with his eyes full of tears and said, "It's the hardest thing I've ever done, because I know he's buried out there somewhere, but it's much too dangerous for a person to venture out in these conditions."

I think of Kyle, my Kyle, buried deep, surrounded by cold and blinding white. I've been digging and digging. I don't know how long I'm supposed to keep digging until it's okay for me to stop trying to find him.

ALICIA: INTUITION

Alicia stands by the front door holding Christy's coat.

"Thank you so much for having us," her sister-in-law says. "The meal was delicious. Everything, perfect."

"Well, I wouldn't say perfect," Alicia says.

"Yes! Perfect!" Christy leans in. "And no surprise guests," she whispers, conspiratorially, in Alicia's ear.

Alicia can't wait for Christy to go home. It's been a peaceful day. Uneventful. Nothing like the baby blessing when Kyle barged in during the sacrament, his hair all disheveled, his eyes wild and frightening. She's sure her extended family has spent many entertaining hours dissecting that whole scene, and she's glad today hasn't provided Christy with any more material.

When Beth moved back home with the baby this summer, Christy had called Alicia, breathless for details. Almost giddy.

"Bipolar?" she asked. "Isn't that the disease you see on television movies where people have all the different personalities?"

Alicia could hardly bear answering; Christy could be so deliberately clueless. "No, Christy," she told her. "It's the disease geniuses sometimes get. Van Gogh. Virginia Woolf. It's a particular struggle for the sensitive and the intelligent."

Today Christy has tried to bring up Kyle and his situation at least half a dozen times. During dessert, she told Alicia she had gone online and looked up lithium, and she said, "It doesn't sound all that bad to me. It's a wonder why he won't stay on it!" Luckily, Beth was out of earshot, upstairs nursing the baby.

Christy's husband, Rob, is outside waiting in the car. Alicia hears him rev the engine.

"You've got a lot on your hands," Christy says. "I don't envy you. A distraught daughter *and* a baby at home! I don't know how you do it."

"We'll be fine, Christy. Don't you concern yourself with us."

Rob honks the horn.

"That's my cue!" Christy says, then reaches over to kiss Alicia on the cheek. She scuttles to the car, carefully balancing her load of Thanksgiving leftovers.

Alicia walks out onto the porch and waves as their Buick rolls around the corner and out of sight. The air is cool against her naked arms. The trees are bare; the ground is brown and dry. November is a terrible month, she thinks.

She wonders if Kyle is hidden somewhere, spying on the house, watching her. She wouldn't be surprised if he were. And it wouldn't frighten her, either. It would mostly make her sad. She wishes she could go back in time eight years to Beth and Kyle's sophomore year in high school, the year they met. Maybe, if she had known what to look for, Alicia could have seen the signs. She could have warned her daughter. Instead of agreeing with Beth, seeing Kyle as interesting and brilliant and emotional, she would have had the good sense to recognize he was more than just a passionate kid. But she was almost as swept up as Beth had been. Here was this boy who came skidding into their lives at full tilt: so smart, so funny, so full of ideas. He'd help Alicia with dinner, doing crazy things like adding Tabasco to the spaghetti sauce and then saying, "Isn't this the best spaghetti you've ever had in your life?" And they'd all agree that yes, yes it was. On Mother's Day he would always send her a card, even before he and Beth married. Sometimes he would write, "Thank you for bringing Beth into this world." Other times, "You're the mother that I never had." Although he did have a mother: an unpredictable, difficult woman who'd raised Kyle all alone. That's where she'd told Beth he should go today.

"He has a mother," she said to Beth. "It's not like we're all he has."

"Yes, we are, Mom," Beth had answered. "And you know it."

But Kyle is not the boy she remembers. The tall, handsome, laughing boy who took her child to the prom, who turned nineteen and dressed up so strikingly in his dark blue suit and served a mission, who came home and said to her and to Nathan, "I would like your daughter's hand." She can't say when the obvious changes started. Six months after Beth married him? A year? The doctors told them diseases like this sometimes come on in early adulthood. There's no way they could have known. But she *should* have known. She feels betrayed—by her own intuition, by God—that she hadn't somehow sensed disaster.

She looks down her normally deserted street and counts the cars lined up along it. Over a dozen are bunched in front of her neighbors' houses. And who are the people that her neighbors have let inside? Grandparents with Alzheimer's, alcoholic uncles, mean-spirited sisters. She knows her neighbors, knows their stories. She knows they have opened their doors on holidays to all sorts of difficult people who come underneath their family umbrellas. But she can't. Not this time. She has kept her door deliberately closed.

The worst part is she doesn't feel guilty for doing it. Because first and foremost, she is a mother. And a mother must protect her child.

BETH: ROMANTIC

From my upstairs bedroom window I can see my mother, coat-less, standing on the porch. She keeps looking up and down the street. I can't help thinking that she's watching for him. Waiting. I told her, chances are, no matter what we say, he'll still show up. But I don't think he'll dare if she's standing right there. He's afraid of her. Only her. Even at the height of his mania she can stop him dead in his tracks.

My mom is a beautiful woman. Prettier than me. She's kept her hair long, just past her shoulders, and she colors it to the same deep reddish brown it was when she was my age. I used to feel sorry for her, that she married my dad. Isn't that funny? I thought she sold out. He was a good dad, sure. Steady, dependable. Nice. But he seemed like an awfully average husband. When was the last time he swept her away on a romantic trip? Wrote her a poem? When I married Kyle, I even wondered if she was jealous.

Kyle's latest romantic gesture was to buy us two one-way tickets to Australia. A few weeks after I had Stella, he came bursting in the door.

"It's a place of mystery! Full of excitement! We can live by the ocean. Live off the land!"

That's when I knew he'd gone off his medication again. I didn't even ask him how he'd paid for the tickets or if we could get a refund. I just silently nodded my head and thought, "I don't think I can do this anymore."

NATHAN: DIRECTION

Nathan wants to get away from the house. It's not that he doesn't love them—his daughters, his sons-in-law, his wife—but by nature he's a solitary man. A lover of quiet. Even now, late in November, he tries to get outside and walk at least once a day. So when Mike asks him if he'll take the grandkids to the park down the block, he's glad for the chance to get some fresh air. He puts the boys in their coats and lets them bolt out the door. He keeps them in sight as they tear down the street, but he doesn't call out to them to slow down or wait or hold hands. He lets them go. He thinks, boys need to run.

It's when he rounds the corner to the park that he sees Kyle in his dusty red Honda, sitting. The engine is turned off and Kyle is staring, immovable, his eyes fixed off in the distance. The boys are at the park now—clambering all over the jungle gym, shrieking on the swings—and even though Kyle is parked just across the street, he gives no indication that he sees them or hears them. His profile stays frozen. Nathan feels suddenly nervous and ashamed, as if he has sneaked up on somebody, as if he's in a place he's not supposed to be. He is unsure if he should gather up the boys and head home. Pretend he never saw his son-in-law. But he has seen him. And even though Kyle hasn't so much as tilted his head, Nathan's sure that Kyle has seen him too.

Nathan sits on the cold metal bench near the swing set. Marnie's boys are hollering, "Grandpa! Watch me slide!" and they don't even recognize their Uncle Kyle sitting across the street in his car, listening and not listening. Watching and not watching. The afternoon sun hangs low in the sky and the wind sends dry leaves skittering across the sidewalk. It's getting chilly. Nathan wonders how long Kyle's been sitting without the car turned on. He wonders if the boy even realizes it's cold.

He's got to go to him. There's no getting around it. No matter what Kyle has done—all the ways he has hurt Beth, all the lies he has told, and his stubborn refusal to stick with the therapy and at least try, at least *seem* to try, to get a hold on this illness that started strangling him so slowly that no one in the family thought to notice until it was out of control—no matter what, Nathan is responsible for this man. He opened his door to Kyle when he was still a kid.

Watched as he burrowed himself deep into their family. And Nathan let him do it. Encouraged it, in his own way. And now he is responsible.

He walks toward the car, his eyes on Kyle's unmoving face. He comes up to the window. Taps it. He can see the shine of tears across Kyle's cheeks.

"Kyle," Nathan says.

Kyle closes his eyes. He keeps his chin set firm.

"Can I just talk to you?"

Slowly, Kyle turns his face to Nathan. He opens his eyes. They are tired eyes, bloodshot and sunken. Weary. He doesn't move to roll the window down.

"What do you want to say?" Kyle asks. His voice is quiet, muffled through the glass.

Nathan considers how to answer this question. That he's afraid for Kyle? Afraid *of* him? That, somehow, he wishes Kyle would disappear and wonders how to save him? That he doesn't know what to say?

Behind him, Nathan can hear his grandsons' voices, clear and brittle in the air.

"Grandpa!" they're calling. "Push us!"

"I just want you to know that you're not alone," Nathan says.

Kyle leans his head back and lets out an angry burst of laughter. "Really?" he says. "You think so? Well you could've fooled me."

It isn't until Nathan is almost to the house that he hears the engine rumble. He doesn't know what it means, if Kyle is leaving or coming. And he doesn't know what he wants it to mean.

He has always been a man of direction. A giver of advice. "Here," he likes to say. "Do this, follow these directions, one, two, three." Then, what had been broken could be fixed. What had been complicated could be understood. He remembers when Beth was a child, how easy it had been to rescue her. If she fell off her bike he could scoop her up, dust off her knees, and kiss her head. Tell her, "Keep trying, keep doing your best—in time it will get easier." But not anymore. She is beyond him. Her life, her story, no longer his.

But he prays for her. For Beth and Kyle and little Stella. They are a family. He asks God to be gentle. It's all that he can do.

KYLE: ELECTRIC

He turns on the car and thinks, stay or go, go or stay, claim your life or run away. Always he's thinking like this. In little poems. Little songs. He's been writing a lot of them down in a notebook that he's brought to show Beth, because sometimes she has such a hard time listening to him, really *hearing* him, and he remembers how she used to love his poems, way back when. He would give them to her, and she would cry and say things like "I love you," like "What would I do without you?" It has been months since he has kissed her, months since he has touched a girl, even, any girl, and he thinks his skin might be starting to go electric with unused tactile energy. He's almost afraid to touch her now. Zap! What if he touched her and an electric current shot out from under his skin and got her? Zip Zap! Maybe it would make her more afraid or maybe it would make her remember the powerful kind of love they share, the very real and, yes, shocking kind of love they have between the two of them. He's always said she's scared because their love is too strong and he is too real. That's why she wants him on that medication, because he's just too real without it, but he's tried to explain that it's the real him she fell in love with anyway and there's no way she'll ever love the other him, the sad, slow, fat, dull—the lurching mannequin he is on those pills. She'll leave him anyway if he takes them. He knows it.

So if she would just take a chance, take a dive with him, go for a ride with him, let her hair flow free and wild with him and love him like she used to, like he knows that she still can. He thinks of Nathan, his face in the window, his sad, pale face. He said, "You're not alone." Not. Alone. If anyone could still be in his corner, it would be Nathan, a good man, a man who maybe sees beyond the surface of things. A kind man. The only father Kyle has ever known. After Stella was born he told Nathan, "I want to be a father just like you." But Kyle was on his meds back then, and even though he kept trying to be a real father—a true man, like Nathan—he didn't have the energy, wouldn't have the energy unless he got rid of the pills, and maybe Nathan understands that. So he hopes Nathan answers when he goes to the door, or Beth, but not Mike, that Minnesota son-in-law with his button-down shirts and his big meaty hand-shakes and his questions—*You got yourself a 401(k)? An IRA? You heard about that IPO?* The last time Mike asked him a question like that, Kyle spelled out his answer, N-O, which he thought was pretty funny, and it flustered that Mike for a minute. If Alicia answers the door, he's brought her the flowers. White roses, her favorite. He doesn't know what he'll say to Alicia—just hand her the flowers and look in her face and hope she recognizes that it's only him, only Kyle, the boy who loves her daughter and loves her family and just wants them to give him a chance.

BETH: IDLING

When my dad came home from the park he told me right away.
"I thought you should know," he said. "He doesn't look well."
I keep thinking, how long? How long has he been around the corner, sitting in his car? All day? Since before the rest of us were even awake? I wouldn't be surprised if he pulled up at four o'clock in the morning. Some nights he sleeps only two, three hours; he gets an idea in his head and he can't stop thinking about it, can't keep himself from jumping out of bed and acting on it. But then, in a way, I knew he was out there too. I could feel him from the minute I woke up.

I step outside our front door. The street is quiet. I hear, very faintly, the rumble of an idling engine. I wait for him.

KYLE: BEAUTIFUL STRANGER

He puts the car in drive, steps on the gas, curves around the corner. Then he sees her standing on the porch, her hands stuffed deep in her pockets, her hair pulled away from her face. She is wearing lipstick, a deep red he has never seen on her before. Her lips are the only color against her pale face. She looks like a woman, like a grown-up. Kyle thinks, This beautiful stranger—she knew I was coming, she's come out to meet me, she's going to welcome me home.

THE PALMERS: PATIENCE

Inside, the family has been warned. Nathan told them, "Kyle's outside, and I think I gave him the impression it's okay to come over." Alicia has gone to her room. Marnie and Tina—the sisters—they both agree it's for the best that he come inside. After all, they argue, what are we going to do? Lock their doors on him forever? Stella's his daughter. It's Thanksgiving. He has a right. Christy and Rob and Grandma have all left, so who does Mom think she needs to impress? It's only Kyle. No matter what, he is still Kyle.

The sons-in-law, Mike and Jimmy, decide to watch football. They will smile at him, say hello. Speak if spoken to.

Beth opens the front door and leads Kyle inside. His face is flushed and spotty. In his left hand, he holds a bouquet of white roses. He lifts his right hand and waves.

"The fam!" he says.

16

Nathan rises from his chair and shakes Kyle's hand. "Good to see you," he says.

"Been a long time," Kyle answers, then laughs once, short and hard.

Marnie says, "Pie! We have pie for you. We have extra. There's plenty."

"Can I take those flowers? Put them in water?" Tina asks.

"Actually, these flowers are for Alicia. And where is my beautiful mother-in-law? The lady of the house. Has she deserted us? Up and flown the coop?"

The sisters look at each other.

"She's resting," Nathan says.

"Or," Kyle says, "is she playing hide-and-seek?"

Outside, the sky is turning dark. Clouds are moving in.

"A storm is coming," Tina says.

"It's a good thing," says Nathan. "We certainly need the moisture."

Everyone nods, earnestly, eagerly. Upstairs, a baby cries.

"There's Stella," Beth says. "I'll go get her."

"No," Kyle says. "No, let me. I mean, can I?"

Beth looks across the room at her father.

"How about you come with me," she says to Kyle. "We can get her together."

They climb the stairs to Beth's old bedroom, Kyle clutching the roses in his left hand. Beth's room is painted butter yellow. It's still decorated like a high school girl's: trophies on the shelves, pictures from school dances. In every photo it's just the two of them, Beth and Kyle. Never anyone else. Different poses and outfits and hairstyles, but always they're the couple with their arms around each other. Heads tilted in close.

Stella's crib has been pushed against the far wall, the only place it will fit. The baby isn't crying loudly. Whimpering, mostly. Patient. Kyle comes to the head of the crib and looks inside. The baby is on her stomach, struggling, pushing up against the mattress with her arms.

"Well look at you," Kyle says.

Stella stops crying at the sound of his voice. Lifts up her head and sees him.

"Look at you so strong," he says to her, his voice gentle, sing-song.

She breaks into a grin.

"How'd you get there on your tummy?"

Then, from the doorway, Beth. "She's on her stomach?" she asks. She walks over to Kyle and stands beside him. They peer into the crib together.

"She really is on her tummy," Beth says. "I was starting to worry she'd spend the rest of her life flat on her back. The doctor said not to worry about her rolling. Said it would come in her own time. But I wondered."

"Sometimes you've just got to be patient," Kyle says.

"True," Beth says. "Very true."

Kyle slides his hand, slowly, along the railing of the crib, until his pinkie touches Beth's. She doesn't move her hand.

"When you love somebody, I mean," he says. "Especially. Patience."

Downstairs, the family is happy to hear about Stella.

"What a champ!" Nathan says.

"She'll be running you ragged before you know it," Marnie tells her sister.

Tina brings Kyle his pie. "I remembered you like pecan," she says.

Kyle sits at the table. He is the only one eating. Someone has turned off the television and the family listens as Kyle's fork clinks against his plate.

"I think I see some flurries," Tina says. "Look. Outside. It's about time."

The family looks out the window. Delicate white snowflakes drift by, lonely, so slow a person could count them coming down.

"It seems, in my day, there used to be so much snow. By Thanksgiving time we'd have had a few good storms. But anymore even the

18

weather's unpredictable," Nathan says. "Can't even count on the weather."

Outside, the flakes twirl in the wind. Kyle has stopped eating his pie.

"I'd like to show my daughter the snow," he says.

The family turns and looks at him.

"Does she have a coat? I'd like to put it on her. Take her outside. Show her the snow. The two of us."

The family looks at Beth.

"You want to show her the snow?" she asks.

"I would like to, yes. Very much. I'm her father."

KYLE: SNOWFLAKES

Kyle sits on the swing at the far end of the yard, holding the baby on his lap. He points at the sky. The baby's eyes follow his finger. He pushes the swing with his feet, slowly. It is not too cold and the breeze is very light. The snowflakes are in no hurry. They spin and tumble and land on the baby's coat. He can't remember ever seeing a snowflake up close, and it looks just as it ought to, symmetrical and complicated and beautiful, the way God likes for things to be. He whispers to the baby, "Look." A snowflake has landed on her sleeve. "Look how pretty." The baby will not look. She keeps her chin tilted up at the sky. The sky is a mystery. And snow. And God. His little daughter understands this. Her tiny hands are getting cold. He covers them with his own. Leans his cheek against her head. Says, "We can keep each other warm."

BETH: WINTER

It is getting dark. I move out to the patio where I can watch them better. Behind me, in the house, I hear my family. I can't pick out

19

what they're saying. I can hear only the tenor of their voices, their laughter and their silences. I bring my legs up and wrap my arms around my knees. Watch my breath turn to white. The swing creaks softly, marking even time.

Between Kyle and me is a path of scattered roses. He didn't drop them all at once. He made himself a trail, like Hansel. He knows I am watching. I can see his silhouette, his dark shadow, rising and falling. His back is to me. He has his arms circled around her.

I listen for Stella's voice. The smallest whisper of sound, the tiniest cry—I will hear it and go to her. The night is that silent. That still.

But then I hear a song, very faint. It's Kyle, and he's singing:

> For health and strength and daily food
> We praise thy name, O Lord.

A primary song. A Thanksgiving song. A short one, sung in a round. I remember singing it with my sisters.

He gets to the end of the line and takes a breath. Begins again:

> For health and strength and daily food
> We praise thy name, O Lord.

I can see his face bent toward the sky. I come up behind him.

"Sing with me," he says. He doesn't look at me. He looks up, and the snowflakes land on his cheeks, his eyelids. "It's such a pretty song. But we have to sing it together."

"Kyle," I say. I reach out for Stella. He keeps swinging.

"For health and strength and daily food," he sings, and waits. This is where I should come in.

"For health and strength and daily food." Again.

I can't sing with him. I listen to the moaning of the swing, the air pushing through the trees.

"Have you ever smelled her hair?" he says. "It smells just like the morning."

He is crying.

"Kyle," I whisper. "Can I have her? Can I have Stella?"

"It's not good to be alone."

"Can I have my baby?"

"I only ask for small things. The song. It doesn't sound right when you sing it alone. It's not complete. It's a very sad song when you sing it all alone."

"She's getting cold."

He stops the swing with his feet. I crouch down beside him, and Stella looks up and smiles. She lifts her arms to me.

"I would give you anything, you know," he says.

"I know," I say, and grasp Stella beneath her arms. Pull her to me.

"We love each other," he says.

He turns to me. His eyes are wide and luminous in the moonlight. His face shines, smooth and white. I reach out and touch his hand. His skin is like ice.

"I've got to get her inside, where it's warm," I say.

"I remember," he says. "You've always been afraid of winter."

"You should come inside too. You're freezing. I can feel it."

He shakes his head. "I don't feel the cold."

"Kyle."

"And the snow is very beautiful."

I leave him out on the swing. I walk with my daughter toward the house, and it's lit up and warm, a deep yellow glow against the night. I hear Kyle's voice rise again in the air, singing, and I hear the creak of the swing and the scuff of his shoes on the hard ground. I don't look back at him. The roses have disappeared in the snow. I tuck my daughter up tight against my chest, open the door, and take her inside.

Tess—1965

ೞ

THINGS UNSAID

He never told her not to go. Tess reminds herself of this as she sits waiting for the bus.

She sits erect, her ankles crossed and knees together, thinking of all her husband has and has not said. Every minute or two she brings her hand up to her hair and smoothes it. Her eyes stay fixed on the dark blue door across the street and two houses down. It is her own house, her own door. She watches, waiting to see if this door will swing open. She considers what would happen if he appeared on the front porch and called out, "Tess," then tilted his head and widened his eyes. She wonders if that would be enough to make her stand, walk across the road, and let him lead her back into the house.

It is a fine morning, the vibrant kind in early fall where nature asserts its will to keep on living: the lawns are cool and green, the sky bright blue. There is no breeze. Tess had seated herself at the bus stop early—it is her first day and she doesn't want to be late—and she wishes she had brought something to read because the few times people have walked past, they appear to be inspecting her. She senses them looking and she has to glance up and then smile, but if she had a book she could keep her head down and pretend not to notice anyone at all.

But of course no one's inspecting her. She is only a woman, sitting, waiting for a bus. A woman holding a brand new canvas bag filled with notebooks and folders and pencils and pens. A forty-year-old woman heading out for her first day of school in twenty years.

She told Joel about her enrollment just three days ago. A terrible mistake to wait that long, she realizes. A simply terrible thing to do to him.

"So you've taken this upon yourself," he'd said. "No discussion. No counsel."

The skin on his face hung slack and pale. He wouldn't look at her.

"Joel," she said. "It was the only way I could think . . ."

"Fine," he said. "I understand."

"No. No, you don't. I didn't want to worry you. I didn't want to make things difficult."

"Difficult, yes. You are right, I am a difficult man. Difficult to talk to. Of course."

She shouldn't have said that word, "difficult." It was a hard word. All those consonants. He struggled and slurred each time he said it.

"It's not you. It's not that I didn't want to talk to you, not that you're difficult. I'm difficult." Tears stung her eyes. "I'm sorry. I never meant to wait so long."

He didn't move to comfort her. "I suppose you feel you must," he whispered, still looking at the ground.

When her acceptance letter from the university had arrived in the mail all those months ago, she meant to talk to him right away. But days passed after she received it, then weeks, yet she couldn't open her mouth. She took a bus to campus and met with her advisor. She registered for classes. She watched Joel as he struggled and hoped for the right day, an especially good day, but none seemed good enough to tell him. Despite everything that had happened, Joel still believed a man should provide. No matter the circumstances. She knew her plans to go back to school to prepare to enter the workforce would be very difficult for him to accept.

So instead of talking to him, she mentally practiced a speech she hoped would soften the blow. "It won't be as bad as you think," she'd hoped to say. "Perhaps if you can concentrate on your rehabilitation and not worry so much about finances, you won't be under so much stress. You'll see some progress."

She planned to explain how she'd earned enough credits from her college days twenty years ago that, after a little over a year of intensive coursework, she'd have her nursing license. How as a nurse she could make a good deal more money than a secretary or a seamstress. How, after graduation, she could find a position that would allow her to work nights, when everyone was sleeping, so no one would miss her and she'd be there for cooking and cleaning and dealing with the children. How she'd always loved the idea of nursing—being a healer, offering others a measure of comfort—and that perhaps she'd even enjoy working. Perhaps they would all be happier.

But when she finally found the courage to tell him—too late, she knows, so late that of course he felt betrayed—she didn't say anything she had planned. Instead, she cried and said she was sorry. Neither one of them has spoken about her decision since. And today, when she said good-bye as he sat at the kitchen table—his oatmeal untouched, the newspaper spread out before him—he didn't answer her. He nodded his head very slightly and didn't look up.

The bus rounds the corner and comes rumbling down the street. She stands, ready, her canvas bag slung over her shoulder. She watches her house, sitting so still and solemn it's hard to believe a person is living inside it. The bus stops and the door sighs open. She pays her fare and finds her seat. Her back is to her house now so she can't watch the door, but she imagines Joel standing there behind it, his hand on the knob he didn't turn.

He said it was love at first sight, and Tess believed him. Even though Arlene Kimball had silky auburn hair and a waist a man could wrap his hands around. Even though Lucille Barker was blessed with eyes as round as buttons and a week's worth of store-bought dresses. Even though Tess saw how these girls and all the others—pretty girls with slim ankles and eager mouths—tipped forward in their chairs to catch every word he said during Sunday School, she never wondered why she was the chosen one. She never felt threatened. She simply believed him.

He became the new Sunday School teacher the day after her twentieth birthday. It was 1945 and he was back in the States, fresh and handsome like so many young men discovering life after war. During the month it took before he asked her to dinner, she never raised her hand in class for fear he'd see it trembling. Instead she sat quietly and studied his face: the cleft in his chin, his strong white teeth, his hair swept back from his brow, curling a bit over his ears. Then when she was afraid she'd been looking too long, she'd close her eyes for just a moment and let his voice ring through her: commanding, sincere, as smooth as caramel. From the first day she heard him speak, she was willing to believe anything he said was true.

On their first date, he told her she was lovely. She had never thought of herself as beautiful, necessarily, but she knew of certain qualities that lent a quiet confidence to her bearing. Her smile was kind. Her pale eyes stood out in contrast to her heavy, dark hair. Her figure was womanly and soft. Still, during that first night out and for many nights afterward, she sat across from him amazed that this man—this real man, twenty-five years old and studying law—had looked into her face and seen something more than smooth skin or full lips. He saw that *she* was something more, something necessary, something that Tess had always hoped she was capable of being but hadn't quite believed she could be until she studied his eyes and decided he couldn't tell a lie.

One month after their first date, Joel proposed.

"I don't have much to offer you," he said as he slipped the slim gold ring on her finger. "Yet."

She didn't mind that there wasn't a diamond. She didn't care that they'd be living in her bedroom at her parents' home until he finished law school. It seemed romantic—delicious, even—bringing him home to her childhood room, closing the door and being alone with him there in her old double bed. But Joel was planning for more. As graduation approached, he sat up with her at night and whispered plans for the life they would build.

"More than you've ever thought to expect," he would say.

Then she would smile and rub his shoulders, happy because he was happy dreaming that way. They were both country children brought to Salt Lake late in their teens, and Tess hadn't been raised to expect prominence or wealth or anything more extraordinary than a home with a nice tidy garden.

"I have all I need," she would tell him. And she meant it.

The professor speaks faster than Tess can write. The other girls in class scratch along in time, their heads bobbing briefly to their papers and up again to their teacher, their expressions dull and slightly sleepy. Tess doesn't understand it. She knows she must look strained—frantic, even—and she feels her heart racing as she scribbles "postoperative care" and then "medical intervention" but has missed how and why the two connect. The phrases hang there on the page, important and bewildering. In the three seconds she has taken to think about this, the professor has again skipped ahead and is now saying something about oral reports. She wonders if she is breathing too loudly and if the young woman beside her has noticed.

College is nothing like she remembered. Her nursing training before she met and married Joel had been challenging, but she doesn't remember feeling so overwhelmed. Suddenly this young version of herself seems farther removed from who she is now than she ever imagined. Of course she should have known how out of touch she would feel. It's the sixties and so much has changed. Yet sitting here surrounded by these fresh young girls, it comes to her swift and hard: she is growing old.

"It will be more difficult than you remember," her mother said, just last week. It made Tess so angry she could scarcely continue the conversation. What did her mother know? When did her mother ever go to school—or deal with a handicapped husband, for that matter? "The mortgage and the medical bills together have almost run through all our savings, Mother," she had wanted to say. "So what do you propose I do? Give up? Let the bank take the house?" Which would kill Joel, she was sure of it. The loss of his home would be his final humiliation. Never, never would she allow it.

But instead of saying this, she told her mother, "Well, now, we'll see. I'm hoping for the best."

And her mother said, "I'll keep you in my prayers."

"Thank you."

"And I'll keep praying for Joel too. For his recovery. Then you won't have to worry anymore and things can go back to normal."

"Thank you, Mother."

"You've got to have faith, you know," her mother said. Commanded. "It's important not to give up on miracles."

"Yes, Mother. I know."

And she does know. She knows all about praying and hope and deep, deep wanting, and yes, she knows sometimes there are miracles. But sometimes there are not.

The professor finishes lecturing, says "Questions?" and waits a beat while nothing but breathing fills the room.

"Until next time then, ladies," he says, and strides away.

The girls begin to chatter. Some laugh, stuffing their notebooks confidently into their bags. Tess stays seated, looking down at her unfinished notes. The classroom empties around her.

Her past is present every day, skirting around her mind like a party balloon trapped along the edges of a high-ceilinged room. Especially at night: she closes her eyes and the past appears, sometimes just a moment stopped in time, but often whole scenes played out with words and smells and sounds. She sees Joel lying on his stomach in the living room, the children wedged around him like puppies, all of them reading comics on Sunday afternoons. She remembers the time she and Joel locked themselves out of the house on Christmas Eve, the way he wrapped her close inside his terry cloth robe, the sound of his rich, throaty laughter as she whispered, "Christy! Let us in!" beneath her oldest daughter's window. She recalls the smell of him before leaving for court: the polish on his shoes, the minty aftershave, the oil he used to slick his hair back, shiny and straight. She would reach down and kiss the top of his head as he read his paper in the morning, and almost always he would lean his head against her, just slightly, and smile up as if to say thank you.

His voice—the way it used to be—comes to her in dreams. Every time it's the same: she stands alone in the center of something, a room or a field or a dark street at night, and she hears him talking. Lines from speeches he gave, or stanzas of poetry, or verses of scripture. Sometimes he's talking right to her, telling her what she should do. "Tess!" he says, "Are you listening to me?" She can hear his voice, but she can't find its source. It is always just behind her. So she turns and turns, his words trailing her around in circles. She wakes up dizzy, her bedspread clutched tight against her chest.

After class she waits in line for the phone. The line is longer than she'd expected, full of young people lolling around, chatting, laughing. She wants to clap her hands sharply like she does with her own dawdling children. Hurry up! Get to it! But these students have no need for urgency. They have no sick husbands waiting gloomily at home, Tess is sure. No unresolved tensions. No things unsaid. Her desire to hear Joel's voice has been building all day, and if she doesn't hear it—even just for a moment, a simple hello so she can read the tone of it—the anxiety clenching inside her will only increase.

Standing two people ahead of her in line is a woman even older than Tess. The woman looks out of place with her tight hair and thick shoes; her face is puckered and concerned. Tess hopes she doesn't look the same way. Even still, she wonders if she should choose this woman as a partner and friend. She'd catch her eye, and just by looking at each other they could find comfort and solidarity. Maybe then this woman's face would relax and they'd both remember what it was like to be young, how it didn't always make things easier. They could remind each other how long these girls will have to wait before they understand the truth about anything.

But today is not the day for new friendships. Today has taken, already, as much energy as she thinks she can muster. Perhaps tomorrow she will go to her. Perhaps next week.

Her turn comes for the phone and, in the space between each ring, she plans what she will say.

"How is your day going?"

Or, "Are you feeling all right?"

Maybe she will say, "I miss you already."

Or just, "I'll be home soon."

But the phone rings twelve times. There are other girls waiting behind her. Class is about to start. She hangs up the phone, but the words she doesn't say remain with her, joining all the others.

This is how she imagines the day of the stroke:

The state capitol sits like a hive atop a great green hill. Inside, well-dressed people are buzzing. Men in gray suits, women in heels and stylish hats, all of them busy and important, clipping past each other, talking in fragments over their shoulders: "Got that?" "Tuesday, then," "I'll check," "Don't forget." The heat and smell of so many human bodies mingles with the sounds of their voices, filling the building with life. It is early afternoon and hundreds of people pass through the rotunda, coming for meetings, leaving for lunch, rushing from office to office, heels ticking along with the second hand of the rotunda clock.

Joel strides through the walnut doors clutching his briefcase. He is almost late for court, so his pace is quick and he brushes past people's shoulders and keeps his eyes fixed straight ahead. From across the room he hears his name.

"Joel!"

It echoes against the marble walls and Joel sees his partner Harry waving, halfway up the staircase.

Joel raises his hand to Harry as if to say, "I see you, I'm coming." Then suddenly he stops. He stands there, still, like the center of a top around which everything else is spinning. He looks down at his feet, then up again, his eyes searching for Harry, his forehead wrinkled with confusion. Then his eyes widen and he opens his mouth and breathes in sharply, as if he's stumbled upon a great surprise or a terrible disaster.

When he drops his briefcase and the papers start to fly, people turn and notice. And when his knees buckle and his body crumples to the floor, the people who are stopped and watching let him fall. The silence starts with Joel and expands, moving in waves across the room, until the quiet has captured them all. The giant clock ticks, and people wonder what to do.

She stands in front of the locked door, panting. She's gone up four flights of stairs, and the room she thought she was trying to find sits dark. The number matches the one on her schedule—403—but she must have made a mistake about the building. The whole floor resonates with emptiness. Everyone else is where they are supposed to be.

She had been nervous about finding this last class of the day. Anatomy is taught in the science building, across campus from where the practical nursing courses are held. She had checked the building, checked the map, gone over the particulars twice or three times. As she entered the building and heard choirs singing, she felt the first flicker of anxiety that she'd made a mistake, but she kept on going up each flight of stairs, still trusting in her planning and double-checking. Now she finds herself in front of a darkened classroom, her stomach twisting with dread. She pulls on the door, just in case.

A long-haired man carrying an instrument case hurries past, his eyes on his walking feet.

It isn't until he starts down the stairs that Tess dares to call out. "Is this the science building?"

He keeps on going down the stairs, his black case slapping against his thigh.

"Excuse me, I'm sorry," she calls, louder.

He stops, turns, says, "You mean me?"

She nods.

"Well this sure isn't the science building," he says. He lifts his case at her and wiggles it by the handle. His mouth is smiling but his eyes are not. "It's way across campus. By the library. Quite a hike."

He turns away from her. She hears the bells from the clock tower ringing. It is four o'clock and she will be late.

She closes her eyes and breathes. She thinks she would like to slide herself slowly down the wall and sit, knees to chin. But she is in public. She's wearing a skirt and pumps. She's forty years old. She keeps standing.

Tess opens her eyes and looks straight ahead, out the window. She sees the broad green lawn and imagines herself walking across it in that way women do when they are hurrying without breaking into a run: her hips swinging, her elbows pumping, her face red and shining with sweat. She imagines herself bursting into that class-room late. The professor will ask her name and she will have to stand there in front of those rows of eyes. They will watch her until he finds her name and marks a little "T" for tardy beside it.

It seems more than she can bear.

She hears the sound of women singing, a choir warming up in-side the building. "Mee–May–Maw–Mow–Moo" they intone, over and over, higher and higher, climbing the scale. She listens as they approach the peak of their voices, notes most people can't reach. Tess herself is an alto and always drops out after high E. But these women are still singing and they must be hitting F or G or even high A.

Every time a scale is completed she thinks they must be finished, but then the piano starts and the voices begin all over again. She imagines the piano going and going, these voices following it without breaking until the notes can no longer be heard.

Outside the window students cross on the lawn. They all walk so quickly. She wonders if they are as certain about where they are headed as they appear, or if they just look that way from this distance, through the glass. She turns to join them.

He is a different man now. Weaker. Angrier. Solemn. A stroke can take many things, but this stroke chose to steal away the power of his voice, the very thing he couldn't afford to lose. Tess read a story in the paper about a sculptor whose hands were burned in a fire. She cut the story out and taped it into her scrapbook so she could read it again and again, proof that God didn't strike just her husband with surgical accuracy. She reminds herself that even Beethoven lost his hearing.

"Upon his rehabilitation," the letter from the firm had said. That's when they would "welcome him back."

Joel had said, "Of course. Of course." He was a litigator, an orator. His voice was what they paid him for.

She doesn't think it will be coming back. It has taken her two years to realize this. The morning after his stroke, she remembers sitting beside him on the edge of his bed, stroking his hair and saying, "The worst is over. Everything gets better from this day on." When Joel opened his mouth to respond and labored for a minute, slurring through one short phrase—"hope you're right"—she still believed it.

Ever since that day she has lain awake at night listening to his vocal exercises, not wanting to fall asleep for fear he would see it as some kind of betrayal. She waits as he sits straight-backed in his office, struggling through poetry, molding his sliding mouth around the consonants. He refuses nursery rhymes. "Last night I stood by the tomb of Old Napoleon, a magnificent sarcophagus of black Egyp-

33

tian marble," she's heard him repeat, hundreds of times. Thousands, perhaps. One night he stayed up until 2:30 until the final syllable of *The Rime of the Ancient Mariner* came out of his mouth in an acceptable fashion. For two years he has struggled through these exercises every night, and nothing has changed.

She wants to say to him, *Joel, what do we need with all those words? The children don't need them; I don't need them. There are ways to go on without them. Let's find these ways together.*

But he wouldn't agree. "If only," he says, and he keeps on battling, waging wars against God, fate, people with their drawn and pitying faces. She wishes she knew which battle he could win. She would help him, if she could.

She is grateful for the bus ride home because it asks nothing of her. All she needs to do is sit. She feels her heart still beating too quickly; all through anatomy class she felt it pound, even though the professor didn't notice she was late. There were at least sixty students in the class. Two more walked in later than she did.

She plans to have calmed herself by the time she reaches home. She wants to come through the door looking the same.

A couple sits in the seat in front of her. The girl rests her head on the young man's shoulder. His arm hangs across the back of the bench and his hand dangles at her neck. His fingernails are ringed in black from oil or dirt or remnants of some kind of hard work, and she watches as the girl brings her manicured fingers up to his and twines their hands together.

The whole ride home Tess watches this couple—the girl leaning her head on the young man's shoulder, his cheek resting in her hair—their bodies bouncing and swaying with the rhythm of the bus. Everyone is quiet.

Six months ago, this was what the doctor told them: "Sometimes if the water is boiling, you've got to take it off the stove."

She remembers Joel sitting on the examining table in his stocking feet, a hospital gown draped over his body. As the doctor talked, Tess watched Joel's face harden, his mouth set firm. He had hoped to be fully recovered by now. But instead of getting better, Joel was weakening. She told him he was pushing too hard, but he didn't want to listen. He refused to go back to the doctor until it became so difficult to get out of bed in the morning, even he couldn't ignore it.

"Your heart is enlarged, Joel. It's dangerous. It's too soon for you to be pushing this hard. You're going to work yourself right to death. You don't need me to tell you this."

But he does, Tess thought. He won't listen to anyone else. Tess knew his job was slowly killing him, but she couldn't get him to quit. He'd started working again—part time, as a law clerk for the Church—and he hated every minute of it. His office was small; his duties were small; his salary was small. At night, he came home gaunt and stony eyed.

"You see these numbers?" the doctor said, pointing to the notation scribbled in red on Joel's chart. "Your blood pressure is dangerously high. There could be a heart attack, another stroke. The only thing you can do for yourself is rest. No more working until these numbers come down."

The doctor spoke briskly, man to man, his eyes right on Joel's face. Joel stayed silent for almost a minute, forming his words.

"Well then," he said.

"If there's anything more I can do," the doctor said, then he grabbed Joel's hand and shook it as if they'd come to some kind of understanding.

Tess stayed quiet while Joel dressed, then followed him out the door. They walked together silently to the bus stop. They had given up their car the previous year—"Another insult," Joel had said—but Tess didn't mind riding the bus. She cared only that Joel minded.

They sat together on the bench, the sound of rushing traffic replacing anything Tess could think to say. When the bus started down the street toward them, they both stood.

35

Joel turned to her.

"I'm sorry," he said.

"About what?"

"Everything. This," he said, and spread his arms wide.

"Darling," Tess said, but the door to the bus hung open, and the driver peered impatiently from under his hat.

Joel waited until she took two steps up inside the bus.

"You go on," he said. "I can't ride this today."

He backed away from the bus and motioned for the driver to shut the door between them. The bus lurched forward and Tess grabbed hold of the cold metal pole. Through the window she could see Joel begin to run. She wanted to yell to him, "Stop, come back, wait for me!" but Joel never could have heard her with the rush of the traffic and the roar of the bus and the thickness of glass between them. Five miles he had to go to reach home. Distance enough to burn right through his heart.

The bus pulled past him as he ran hard along the sidewalk. She thought she could hear him going, the sound of his feet against the ground, sharp as gunfire.

She stands in front of her lighted house. It is six o'clock, just when she said she would be home from school, and she is glad to be on time. The children have a dinner planned—so sweet of them, and so perceptive, since they know as well as Tess that Joel hates having his meals delayed. She's sure they won't keep it up, but for tonight their gesture means the world. She stops on the sidewalk and looks through the tree branches into the dining room. Although she can't see him, she imagines Joel sitting at the head of the table, waiting.

She notices their daughter Christy moving in from the kitchen, bringing a steaming dish to the table. Nathan follows behind her carrying milk poured into a glass pitcher. She hears a loud burst of Russell's laughter.

She thinks of these children, their good hearts and all they have lost, all they are asked to do, and she wants to gather them to her soft body and ring them inside her arms. But they are teenagers now, growing and grown, all angles and corners, their changed voices echoing through her home.

She stands in the twilight. A breeze blows by and two yellowed leaves pirouette through the air, circle one another and land silently at her feet. She listens to her children's muffled voices rising and falling, one on top of another, almost like a song. She wonders if this is what they sound like every night when people pass them by. She wonders if anyone else has noticed it is beautiful.

Last night, he came to bed without doing his exercises.

"In bed so soon?" she asked him, and he nodded. Then he turned away from her, his back stiff and straight. She lifted her hand above his shoulder, wanting to touch him. She listened to his low breathing. Her hand stayed still in the air.

"You are a good man," she said. "You're doing all you can. We know this, every one of us."

He inhaled slowly and held it.

"We're your family," she said. She laid her fingers lightly on his arm. He let out all his breath.

All during dinner, the children ask about her day.

"What was it like?" they ask her. "Who did you meet? What did you learn?"

Joel follows the conversation, turning his head from one side of the table to the other.

"It was interesting," Tess answers. "It was different. I'm glad to be home."

Christy made biscuits and chicken, Joel's favorite, and when Tess catches her eye to show her how grateful she is, her daughter blushes down at her plate, embarrassed and proud.

Tess starts clearing the table and tells the children, "You have the rest of the night off." They scatter—Christy to her room, Nathan and Russell outside. Joel stands and brings Tess his plate then walks to the living room window, his hands in his pockets, watching his boys play catch on the lawn.

Tess stays at the sink, her hands in the warm soapy water. Autumn comes in through the open kitchen window. The night is especially fragrant and cool, and she is grateful for fall, how it reminds her to pay attention to things.

They stand a room apart, Tess at her window and Joel at his. She can feel the air moving between their turned backs.

"This wasn't how . . ." he says, and stops. She turns from the sink and sees him, the dusky evening light lined around his silhouette, his shoulders slightly bent.

She moves in behind him. Slowly she wraps her arms around his waist, rests her head against his back.

"It will be all right," she says. "No matter what."

She can feel him trembling beneath her cheek. During all this time of disappointment and trial, she has never seen him cry. She waits, holding him, until she feels his breathing steady and his heartbeat slow. Then he turns to face her.

"I'm trying," he says. "Every day."

She looks into his face. "I believe you. So am I."

He takes her hand, brings it up to his heart and holds it there for a moment, squeezing it tight. She wants to say something more. That she loves him, still. That she's sorry. But they both remain quiet. Finally, he leans in and kisses her forehead. When he pulls back and releases her hand, she is grateful she didn't say more. The silence is full enough for both of them.

He turns and heads up the stairs to his office. Tess hears the familiar scrape of his high-backed chair, the rustling of papers, and soon his voice comes from behind the door.

"'It is an ancient Mariner,'" he begins.

The sky is darkening. It is time for her boys to come inside where it is warm and safe. She leans out the open window and calls their names. "Come on home," she says, and her voice is loud and strong, riding on the air.

Her canvas bag sits in the entryway. Tonight, while her children sleep, she will open it. She will sit on the front room sofa and spill out all her new books. She will turn their pages and learn about muscles and bones. She will remember the organs she studied so many years ago—what they do and why. It will be comforting to know the names of all the vital things; she will memorize everything the body uses and needs, and never forget it.

Joel's voice trails steadily down the stairs. She will stay here, reading, until he finishes, his voice working through the final stanza:

> He went like one that hath been stunned,
> And is of sense forlorn:
> A sadder and a wiser man,
> He rose the morrow morn.

Nathan—1981

ȣ

A BED OF YOUR OWN MAKING

Nathan is running late. Heart thumping, face flushed, rushing, worried, ears attuned to the sound of the garage door rising. He has the bed he's built fitted together tight and the mattress on, so the room isn't a complete mess, but he has shoved the old metal frame out into the hall, and the sheets and pillowcases are still in the dryer. He threw in an armful of the kids' laundry for good measure, and the buckles on Tina's overalls chink against the side of the dryer drum, ringing off the seconds like a timer. He started the laundry two hours ago, back when it seemed a great idea to wash the sheets *and* do a load of the girls' clothes (wouldn't she be impressed!), but, as usual, time has gotten away from him. And now it's five fifteen. Alicia is due home from her hair appointment any second and Nathan is frantic and sweaty and angry at himself, fearing he's jeopardized the moment he's envisioned all these months just because he thought clean sheets would be the capper. Now she may not even be able to get down the hall to the bedroom.

From the beginning he underestimated how long it would take. Counting backward to the day Alicia gave him the idea, nine months have passed. Time enough to start and finish a whole school year. Grow a baby. And in all this time she hasn't figured out what he's up to. Sometimes he thought she could sense it. They would be alone together—standing in their pajamas in the bathroom, brushing their teeth, taking turns spitting into the sink—and he would be afraid to meet her eyes in the mirror for fear she would see a secret there, and wonder. But now the day is here and he's quite confident he's pulled it off. He's done a thing she never would have expected of him. He's built a bed. For her. A surprise bed, done just in time for her thirtieth birthday.

It was winter when he thought to build it: fiercely cold, the wind blowing against the house in rattling gusts, the kind of night that sent Nathan and Alicia to bed early. Such storms were one of Nathan's favorite parts of winter. They reminded him how safe he and his family were in their own warm house, how peaceful against the cold and wind and snow.

He sat in bed, reading. Alicia lay beside him, her book spread open on her chest, her eyes fixed off in the distance. A pale circle of light from the bedside lamp fell against her face, shadowing the hollows of her cheeks.

"Three more pages," he said, and she nodded.

He read a few paragraphs and turned the page, but he could feel her beside him, tense, her waiting a palpable energy in the room. He hurried, skipping past dialogue, rushing toward the end of the chapter. But still she couldn't wait until he closed his book.

"Do you ever wonder who's in charge?" she asked. Her hand rested on her stomach, bulging slightly beneath her nightgown. "Who decides how things turn out? I mean, *is* it God? Sometimes I wonder if he's just watching, not mixing himself up in any of this. Like our lives are just a big play, and he's waiting to see what happens next. Wouldn't we feel a little silly, then? After we die, I mean. Here we've been praying and asking and trying to do his will, and what if he doesn't have a hand in our fate, after all? What if he just ends up patting us on the back and saying, 'Thanks for the great show!'"?

Nathan bent back a triangle on the page to mark his place, shut his book and laid it on the table beside him. He knew what was making her talk this way. It was the baby. Their two girls were seven and five, and for a while he wondered if Alicia would ever get pregnant again. They'd never practiced birth control. But as time went on and Alicia failed to conceive, instead of being upset, as Nathan assumed she would be, Alicia seemed quietly relieved. When this pregnancy came, Alicia said all the right things about being excited and feeling blessed to add another child to the family. But Nathan had his doubts about her sincerity. And he'd been too afraid to ask.

"What if it is okay to just say, 'Hey, God, *I* pick. *I* choose.' What if that's completely, entirely okay, and we just don't know it?" Her cheeks were flushed, her voice trembling.

Nathan took a deep breath. He wasn't good at these conversations, never had been. He had a hard time understanding Alicia's eagerness for complication.

"I think it is okay, Alicia. That's what free agency is all about. That's why we're all here: to choose." He turned onto his side and put his hand atop hers. The baby was still too small for him to feel as it kicked and squirmed, but he could imagine it under there swimming around. Growing. Turning into a person he was excited to meet. "So I choose to stop worrying and be happy and go to sleep."

"But do you realize we're not young anymore? I mean, look at me, Nathan. Really look." She pulled her hair back from her face with one hand and gazed at him with worried eyes.

Nathan tried to recall Alicia's features as they'd once been, the face he knew back in college: round and smooth and bright. Although in many ways she was prettier than she'd ever been, she was right. She wore a certain weariness now, around her eyes.

"Beautiful as always," Nathan said.

"That's not what I mean!" Her voice was sharp and impatient. "I just feel like I'm at the mercy of everything and everybody, you know? Almost thirty years on this earth, and I wonder if I've ever made a decision that's mine. Not a have to, a supposed to, a need to. But a *want* to. A choice."

You chose me, Nathan wanted to say. Didn't you? But he reminded himself that she was pregnant, she was emotional. She always got this way when she was expecting, saying things she didn't really mean. He knew there was even science to back up this behavior, what with all the changes in her body chemistry. It was his job to be patient and supportive.

"You'll feel better in the morning," he said. "You need some sleep."

She looked up at the ceiling and shook her head.

"Never mind," she said.

"What?"

"Just, fine. Okay?" She briskly brushed away a tear. "I'm always tired. Sleeping isn't going to change that. What you want me to do is stop talking. So I will."

She whipped around onto her side, her back to Nathan.

"Honey," he said. "Hon."

"No. Never mind. We're done." She reached up and snapped off the lamp.

He looked outside, into the darkness. Snow flung itself at the window and the house shook against the wind. Alicia lay taut inside the covers, stiffened against him, and he could tell by her breathing she was a long way from sleep. What did she want from him, he wondered? What did she need? If he could have chosen his life, he would have wished to be born a hundred years before his time, as a farmer or a rancher. He would come home to his family at the end of the day with dirt and sweat all over him, the evidence of his work and good intentions rubbed fast into his skin. All his life he'd been a quiet person, tentative, polite. "You're a gentle man," Alicia had told him when they were dating. "A gentle man, and a gentleman." He had taken it as a compliment, as it was intended to be. But to be a capable man. To be the one who made life better. It was all he ever wanted.

But what could he do for her, really? What could he change? He taught high school history. They barely squeaked by, but she knew this was how it would be when he decided to major in education, and she was okay with it. She had promised him. But weren't they happy? As happy as they had a right to expect?

His eyes adjusted to the dimness and he looked around the room. Alicia had tried her best to make it pretty with light blue curtains and a quilt she tied herself. But it wasn't a beautiful room. Their chest of drawers was old and scuffed, a garage-sale buy that still smelled faintly of shoe polish and cigarette smoke. And they didn't even have a headboard—just an old metal bed frame. They leaned up against the wall to read. Every once in a while he would catch Alicia looking in the Sunday ads at the bedroom sets, but never once had she asked for anything new. He remembered her complaining about George and Diane, their neighbors across the street, after Diane spent the afternoon showing off some new furniture. "From Ethan Allen!" Alicia had told him. "Who spends money like that on a headboard and a dresser?"

But he'd seen the envy in her eyes. They weren't the types who would spend that kind of money. *Could* spend that kind of money. He looked over at his wife, so small inside the covers, her dark hair spread across the pillow. She was still awake, he was sure of it. He should reach over and touch her shoulder, say "Talk to me," say "I'll listen." But he couldn't do it. He knew, no matter what he said, it would be wrong.

But maybe there was something he could do. And then she would remember why she chose him. Then she could be happy.

At 5:17 the dryer stops clanging, so Nathan bounds down the basement stairs to the laundry room. He flings laundry on the floor and picks through the T-shirts and pajama bottoms and underwear until he finds the top and bottom sheets and counts—one, two, three, four—pillowcases, his heart thumping with adrenaline and the expectation that he just might pull this whole thing off in time. As he jogs past the upstairs window, he checks the curve in the road and doesn't see her Toyota coming, and now he's quite sure he can do it. The sheets are warm and smell mountain fresh—just as the box claims they should—and as he snaps them in the air and watches them billow down smooth across their brand new bed, he's convinced he's never had a better idea in his life.

He holds each pillow under his chin as he stuffs it into its case, then arranges them—blue, green, blue, green, just how Alicia likes them—against the gleaming headboard. He tucks the edges of the bedspread down, then steps into the hall. He walks inside the room again and lifts his head, wanting to take it all in as if it were a surprise to him too, and he's so impressed with the way the room has been transformed, he gives himself the chills.

The bed fills up the center of the room. He picked a dark cherry stain that makes the wood look rich and expensive. The four posts measure as thick as his thigh, and each groove on the headboard stands precisely one inch from the groove before it. He has run his hand over every surface of this bed, and it is entirely smooth and cool. He stands with his arms folded over his chest, examining the work wrought by his own two hands, and possibilities expand inside him like a full, deep breath.

Five more minutes is all he needs. Five more minutes, and everything will be perfect. It's possible Alicia could be running a little late. This "Beauty Day" is a gift from Nathan's mother, and the certificate had said, "Manicure, Pedicure, Hair: The Works!!" He hopes she is relaxing. Taking her time. Nathan's the first to admit that, since the new baby, she hasn't had a minute to herself. She's been excited about the beauty day for weeks.

"This is the first real haircut I've had in years," she said. "Maybe I should finally chop it."

This is one of those exchanges Nathan recalls because it was so fraught with trouble. He remembers Alicia sitting at the dining room table organizing bills. She took a big clump of hair in her fist and wagged it at him.

"I think I'm going to let them cut it off. I'm thirty. It's about time. Don't you think it's about time?"

He considers now how he should have answered this question. But he can't lie: even after eight years of marriage, he loves to watch her walking away from him so he can see her hair swing, glossy and alive across her back.

So what he said was, "You mean cut it *off* off? Like, short?"

She sighed. "How did I know he'd have a problem with this?" she said into the air.

"Hey, whoa," Nathan said. "There's no problem here. I'm just asking. Just wondering. I mean, Alicia, it's your *hair*, after all. I thought you loved your hair. Everybody loves your hair."

"Hair, hair, I'm sick to death of all this hair. Do you know what it's like washing this hair every day, blowing it dry, keeping the kids from pulling on it and yanking it out? Do you know how much time I spend cleaning the bathroom alone, Nathan? Hair in the sink, hair on the floor. Do you have any idea what it's like to get down on your hands and knees in the bathroom every morning while Beth is screaming and Tina is whining and Marnie is begging for snacks and pick up all those hairs? You have no idea, Nathan. Really. None."

Here is the irony: regardless of whether her hair short or long or in-between, Nathan worries more that Alicia is *too* beautiful, rather than not beautiful enough. Even now, after three children—just four months after having her third baby, for heaven's sake!—she still turns heads. When they met at BYU they were both attractive in a simple, rosy-cheeked, healthy kind of way. But as the years have passed Alicia has grown leaner, more angular and interesting. Even her hands seem to have lengthened and tightened. Sometimes, when she's sitting beside him in the car or they're watching television together, he secretly takes her in: the shape of her lips, the line of her jaw, the smooth white skin along her collarbone, and he thinks to himself, "Here is a beautiful woman." He is not sure if he deserves a woman as beautiful as this. Nathan, himself, has grown a bit puffy with age. His hairline is receding. But whenever they talk about sex, Alicia tells him he is not the problem.

"It's not you," she has said to him, over and over. "It's not that I don't want to have sex with *you*, Nathan. It's that I don't want to have sex period."

Nathan has tried to believe her, but it's hard. She has cited hormones, sleep deprivation, lack of time to herself. One night when she was angry she said, "You try having hands all over you all day and see how you like having hands all over you at night." She has even told him she doesn't feel sexy, which made no sense to him at all.

So he hopes the bed isn't too obvious. If she asks, he can tell her honestly that it didn't start out as some romantic ploy. And knowing his wife, the Freudian connection will never occur to her, anyway. To Alicia, a bed is for sleeping.

It is 5:20 and in the last two minutes Nathan has managed to gather up the old metal frame and drag it to the girls' room. He'd hoped to have time to bind it up nicely with duct tape and store it in the eaves of the garage, but Marnie, Tina, and baby Beth are having a sleepover at his mom's, so he figures it's okay to leave it there in a heap for just one night.

In the seven years since Marnie's birth, Alicia hasn't been apart from her girls overnight even once. Most nights, in fact, one of the three of them ends up in Nathan and Alicia's bed. Even though Alicia sometimes complains about the lack of sleep, Nathan sees her in the mornings, lying there with Beth curled up against her chest, Alicia's nose buried in the sweetness of her baby's fine hair. He sees how she wraps her arms around Tina—who's getting so gangly now—holding her tight as a pillow. He remembers that as newlyweds she wanted to cuddle with him while they slept, lie there with his arms around her waist and their legs intertwined, but he told her he just couldn't sleep that way. It was too hot, too claustrophobic, made him sweaty. He didn't mean to hurt her feelings. From that time on he would reach one leg out across the middle of the bed so his foot touched her calf, just to let her know it wasn't personal.

But tonight. Tonight! For the first time in way too long, he will have her all to himself. He will hold her, if she wants him to. They can sleep curled up against each other and wake up to nothing but silence and possibilities. Happy together, in a bed he made himself. The bed he'll pass down to his children. He imagines he and Alicia grown old together, telling the story of this bed to their grand-children, saying, "This bed will be yours someday." He sees half a dozen or so little round heads—the future heads of the Palmer family—nodding in solemn appreciation and understanding.

He reminds himself not to get carried away.

Because he realizes that, potentially, he's created a problem for himself. All the time and worrying, the attention to detail, the plan-ning of one step and the next and the next, and suddenly it's not just a bed he's built but a monument. And he understands—he fears—that for Alicia it could simply be a bed. In her mind this bed has never existed before; it's a surprise that he has built, set up, and pushed tight against their bedroom wall. A pretty thing. A nice thing for a husband to do. He imagines her saying, "It's so *sweet* of you, hon," which she very likely could say, but this is not the response he wants from her. In his most optimistic imaginings he pictures her with tears welling in her wide eyes, her hand to her mouth in speech-less gratitude. He sees her reaching out her long fingers, running them across the smooth surface of the footboard. Sometimes he even en-visions her falling backward on the bed, her arms loose and wide, her face tilted up at him, full of satisfaction.

"Come here," he imagines she will say. "Come join me."

This is what he wants. He doesn't know what he will get.

It is 5:25. Everything is in place. He eases himself onto the mat-tress, sitting straight and stiff, not wanting to wrinkle the bedspread. Wanting to look prepared. After all these months—working out time to spend in his buddy Carl's woodshop at school; going to Ethan

Allen with a measuring tape; cutting, nailing, sanding, staining—this is the moment. He's done it. He's ready. He waits.

At 5:33 he finally hears the garage door lift and her car pull into the driveway. His heart speeds in his chest. The lock clicks open, and her shoes thump against the wall as she kicks them off in the entryway. He hears her footsteps on the stairs.

The bathroom door opens and closes. He thinks he hears a shuddering intake of breath.

"Alicia," he decides to say. No response. Then again, louder.

"Alicia! Hon! Come into the bedroom. It's a surprise!"

Silence.

This isn't like her. She almost always calls hello when she comes through the door, and she never—almost never—fails to respond directly.

But he doesn't want to get up and go to her because it would ruin the choreography of it all. He doesn't want to drag her in by the arm, point and say, "Look here." He wants her to walk in and see him and the beautiful new bed—both of them together. He's imagined the scene so many times it seems the only way to do it right. He calls out again.

"Hon? Alicia? Just come here for a sec. You'll love it. I promise."

"Stop. Ordering. Me. Around." Each word echoes against the ceramic tile.

He realizes this may be an emergency. He plays it wrong and the whole night is ruined. He hurries off the bed and goes to the bathroom door. Locked. He shakes the handle.

"Alicia, hey, let me in. I'm worried now."

She's crying. He can hear it. *Why?* He wants to ask her. *Why now?*

"Alicia," he says again.

She sighs, long and loud. Finally he hears the click of the door unlocking. He opens the door and sees Alicia on the toilet, her arms wrapped around her head as if she's protecting herself from blows.

"What is it?" he says softly, and squats down beside her.

50

"A terrible, terrible mistake," she sobs.

"Whose mistake? Are you hurt? Is everybody okay?"

"You were right, okay? Like always, so you don't even have to say it. Trust me, I already know."

"Alicia, hey, just look at me. All right?"

She lowers her arms from around her head and lifts her face to his. Her cheeks are red and blotchy.

"See?" she cries. "See?"

Her hair is cut short above her collar. It flips up on the ends and little layers frame her thin face. She looks like a pixie.

"You mean your hair? It's actually kind of nice. Cute, I mean. You look cute."

She rolls her eyes. "You *have* to say that, of course, since I'm your wife and I'm in here having a nervous breakdown. And I'm thirty. And I look awful. Awful!"

She lowers her head into her arms and sobs again. She looks so small and fragile, folded in on herself. He rubs her upper arms, tries to will her to look up again, to see his face and know that everything is okay. It has to be okay, today of all days.

"It's not the end of the world," he says, which immediately seems like a stupid thing to say. He reaches up and strokes her bowed head. "See? It feels real soft and nice. You'll like it, just wait. You'll get used to it."

She pulls her breath in slowly and holds it. Her blue eyes shine electric through her tears, so beautiful when she's been crying.

"But I'm nothing that I thought I would be. See?" she says, and spreads her arms wide. "What is this? What am I?"

This, he thinks, is quickly becoming one of those fraught conversations. A minefield. He must step very, very carefully.

"You're . . . you're beautiful. You're smart. Alicia, you're a great mom. You're my wife."

"Yeah, right," she says, and wipes her nose with the back of her hand. "I bet you thank your lucky stars for that one every night."

"But don't you know I love you?," he asks.

She smiles a slow, sad smile, then breathes deeply and closes her eyes.

"I'm just so tired," she says. "Just really, really tired."

He circles his arm around her shoulders and walks with her into the bedroom. She keeps her head buried deep into the side of his chest and doesn't look up. He pulls back the covers, and as she begins to lower herself onto the bed she notices.

"Nathan. How?"

She reaches out her hand just as he had hoped she would and runs it along the headboard.

"How?" she says again.

"I worked the time in here and there."

"You did this? You built this?"

"I did. Yes."

She covers her face with her hands and begins to cry again. Nathan waits for her to finish, to raise her head and smile, but she keeps on crying.

"Surprise!" he says, hoping she'll look up at him and laugh.

Instead she speaks into her hands, "I'm sorry, I'm sorry."

Nathan walks around to the other side of the bed, the side near the window, and leans his head against the cool pane of glass. He looks across the street at George and Diane's house. He wonders if the two of them are inside, and if so, what they are saying to each other. How they are saying it.

He sees Alicia's reflection in the window. She's lying on top of the bedspread, her back curled away from him. The crying has stopped. He eases himself onto the edge of the bed beside her. He rests his hand on her shoulder, then pats it slowly, as if consoling a child.

"I ruin everything," she says into her pillow.

"Nothing is ruined. It doesn't have to be ruined."

"You can't go back, Nathan. You can't rewind and start everything over again."

Outside their window there is evidence of life—kids playing, cars rolling by—but in the dim light of afternoon, it seems to Nathan

52

the day is finished. He wants to say something more, to argue with her, but she is right, they can't go back. Things get created and they can't get unmade. As he sometimes tells his students: History writes itself fast, so swiftly you hardly realize it's happening, till you look behind you and there's enough to fill a book.

"Lie with me," she tells him, so he does what she says, tucking in behind her, wrapping his arms around her chest. She feels weightless and brittle in his arms, like papier-mâché. Her heart beats quick as a bird's. Soon Alicia's breathing begins to lengthen and slow, and Nathan closes his eyes, matches his breathing to hers. With each exhalation, Nathan can feel her neck loosen against his chest. Her hands, fisted beneath his own, uncurl. She relaxes into sleep.

Nathan lies awake beneath his closed eyes, breathing in the chemical sharpness of Alicia's hair, the smell of fresh stain on the headboard. He runs his hand along the length of his wife's bare arm. It is entirely smooth and cool.

Marnie—1983

☙

SUNDAY STORY #1:
TRUE

As a child, Marnie knows a lot of things. She knows her father is kind and strong and can be counted on. She knows her mother works hard to do what's right. She knows being the oldest of three sisters, and smart, means she must shoulder her fair share of responsibility. She knows living in America makes her lucky. She knows God talks to people. She knows everything happens for a reason. She knows the Church is true.

Today is the first Sunday of the month, fast Sunday, and she likes getting up during testimony meeting and telling people what she knows. She stands among the folding chairs in the overflow of the Taylorsville 25th ward chapel, waiting her turn. She is nine years old, pale and slim shouldered, her long dark hair braided tight and circling the crown of her head as if she were a princess. The deacon with the microphone is coming at her slowly, dragging the cord behind him. She wonders if he's seen her; if it's her turn, yet, to talk. She stands on tiptoe and tries to catch his eye, but he is looking off to the left, two rows ahead of her. The deacon hands the microphone to Brother Sorensen, who is short and slim, the creases standing sharp along the length of his pants. His hands tremble, and for a few moments no sound comes from him but unsteady breathing. The members of the congregation have shifted in their seats, dozens of heads craning backward, eager eyebrows lifted, children hushed, waiting for him to tell the story that they all know is coming. And he tells them: how his daughter, three years old, fell off the bunk bed the week before, hitting her head; how he and his wife heard the crash and came running; how lying there so still, she seemed as if she were dead, but Sister Sorensen put her hand underneath her pajama top and onto her chest and said, "She's warm, she's breathing. I can still feel her heart." How at the hospital when he blessed her, he felt the presence of God in the room. How she improved through the night and finally opened her eyes. How he is grateful to all of them, for their phone calls and meals and offers of support, but mostly he is grateful to God for his kindness, since he is a weak man and not very deserving.

Marnie watches all the people watching him and she can see how they love him. She notices her father's eyes are bright and wet. This feeling in the room—this fullness, this quiet—she knows is the Spirit.

Brother Sorensen sits down, and the deacon comes toward Marnie now with the microphone. She stands. She tries not to stand up every testimony meeting because, even though she is a child, she understands her tendency to wear people out. But there are times, like today, when the knowledge of things as they are is so heavy and real that she can feel it pressing taut inside her skin, struggling to get out. She has heard people say their hearts pound just like hers does, prompting them to stand and speak. "I would be ungrateful if I didn't stand," they explain, and Marnie agrees with them. She doesn't want to be ungrateful.

Marnie grasps the microphone.

"I'd like to bear my testimony," she says. "I know this church is true."

She notices the heads turning back around and away from her as people shift in their seats to face forward again. This ward knows Marnie, knows what she will say—what she always says—and while it's charming and sweet, it is hardly dramatic. They get back to shushing their children, thumbing through their lesson manuals, closing their eyes.

But Marnie's testimony keeps going. "I know," she says, again and again. When she finishes and sits back down, her father covers her knee with his hand.

Tina—1985

୧୪

SUNDAY STORY #2: TOGETHER FOREVER

Tina hates Primary singing time. First because she hates singing. She always has. She's terrible at it, and it doesn't help that her big sister Marnie's got "the voice of an angel," or so their mom says. Lately, though, singing in Primary has been driving her particularly crazy. Like today. Sister French, the music leader, has drawn a house on a piece of poster board and cut out little windows and doors that swing open. Behind each one is the title of a song about families. Nearly every kid in senior Primary has a hand in the air, almost ready to burst because they *really really* want to get picked to open one of those silly little cardboard doors, and Tina just doesn't get it. Even Marnie's waving her hand in the air and she's *eleven*, which means she should be so over these baby games by now.

"Marnie, you've been singing so well," Sister French says. "How about you come and pick the next song?"

Tina watches her sister flounce down the aisle and she fights the urge to stick her leg out and trip her. She looks at the clock. Eight more minutes until the torture is over and they get to go to home.

"Oh, you've picked one of my favorites!" Sister French exclaims. "It's 'Quickly I'll Obey'!"

The babiest of baby songs, Tina thinks. Maybe Beth and the kids in junior Primary should be singing it, but it's beyond ridiculous to think any respectable nine-year-old would dignify the song by opening her mouth. She turns to Stevie Moody in the seat beside her; he's a quiet kid but one she likes because he lets her use his bike jump.

"This song is so bogus," she whispers. She just learned the word—bogus—and she's been using it a lot. She likes the way it bursts out of her mouth, almost like a swear but not. Stevie nods at her gravely.

Marnie heads back to her seat and the senior Primary starts singing. Tina can hear her sister's voice, loud and clear above the others':

When my mother calls me,
Quickly I'll obey.
For mother knows just what is best
Each and every day.

It's the perfect song for Marnie to pick, Tina thinks. They should rename it "Marnie's Song," or "Marnie's Anthem"; her sister could have everybody play it for her before she enters the room, like that song for the President.

Then she feels something sharp jab her side. She turns and looks over her shoulder and it's Marnie, leaning in from the row behind to poke her with a pencil.

"Stop it!" Tina hisses.

"Then sing!" Marnie hisses back.

The second verse starts. Now it's "When my *father* calls me." Tina clamps her mouth shut and twists around to face her sister. She widens her eyes and bobbles her head back and forth, mocking the rhythm of the song.

"I'm telling Mom," Marnie whispers.

Tina slaps her palms against her cheeks and makes her mouth a perfect O.

"Tina?" It's Sister French. "Is there something you'd like to share with us?"

Tina whips back around in her seat. She can't afford getting in trouble in Primary again; her mom said one more time and she's grounded.

"No," she says, looking down at her feet.

"Perhaps you can help me out, then," Sister French says. "Pick the next song."

Tina has to do it. Last time she was grounded she couldn't watch TV *or* listen to the radio, and the only books her mom would let her read were those comics based on the Book of Mormon. She sighs and slumps her way to the front of the class.

"Pick a window," Sister French says. "Any one."

Tina can't look anybody in the face, she's so embarrassed. There are two whole windows left. *What a challenge!* she thinks. She chooses the one next to Marnie's and bends back the flap.

"Would you like to read the title for the rest of the Primary to hear?" Sister French asks.

"'Families Can Be Together Forever,'" Tina mumbles.

"What's that?" Sister French asks. "Louder, please."

"'Families Can Be Together Forever,'" Tina says, maybe a bit too loud this time.

"This is such a great song," Sister French says. "And we only have time for one more, so lucky you picked it!"

Tina stands at the front of the room, frozen, expressionless.

"You can sit down now," Sister French says, giving Tina a little nudge between her shoulder blades. As Tina heads for her seat, Sister French starts waving her arms. The children sing the familiar lyrics about Earthly families living together in heaven eternally—how, through Heavenly Father's plan, moms and dad and uncles and aunts and cousins and grandmas and grandpas and every single person you care about (well, every single person you care about who's righteous enough) gets to spend all of forever together. Tina imagines this version of heaven as very happy and busy, like a huge family reunion with lots of activities, but where no one is allowed to be grouchy or annoying or sad.

"Families Can Be Together Forever" is one of Tina's mother's favorite songs. Just last Monday night they all sang it for family home evening, and her mom asked them, "Doesn't this song make you grateful to know that we'll always be together?"

Tina remembers both Marnie and Beth nodding and smiling, but the question made Tina sick with dread. She knew from her Primary lessons about the three degrees of glory: celestial, terrestrial, and telestial. She knew only the best of the best went celestial, and what were the chances she'd wind up in there? She even asked her Primary teacher, "What if somebody in your family isn't good enough to make it to the celestial kingdom? Would they be all alone, then?"

"Well no unclean thing can enter into heaven, that's for sure," her teacher answered. "But maybe the good family members can go down and visit the other ones, if they feel like it."

"But what if they don't feel like it?" Tina asked.

"That would be a good reason for people to make sure they keep the commandments, then, wouldn't it?"

For months after that lesson, Tina's been trying to work up the courage to ask her dad to promise he'll come visit her once they're all dead, but she can't make herself say the words. Because then he'll know for sure she's a sinner. She'd been clean and pure for a few weeks, at most, after her baptism when she was eight, but since then she's racked up an impressive list of sins: taking a dollar off her dad's nightstand and buying dangly silver earrings she can only wear in secret; kicking Marnie in the shin when she wouldn't break her popsicle in half and share; and, just yesterday, flipping the bird at Mike Drummond when he called her a greasy-haired tomboy. The worst part of yesterday's sin was that the look on Mike's face made Tina *glad* she'd done it. She didn't feel one bit sorry at all. She couldn't imagine anybody else in her family even thinking of flipping the bird, let alone liking it. Even her dad could never understand.

"Let me hear you!" Sister French exclaims. "Good and loud, like you mean it!"

Tina tries, but the tune gets stuck in her throat. She can hear Marnie's voice behind her, though. Sweet and pure as an angel's.

Beth—1986

ℭℬ

Sunday Story #3:
Helpful

When Beth gets home from church on Sunday, she decides she's going to try her best to be helpful. Earlier today, in Primary, she had a lesson about helping. All the kids in her CTR 5 class made little wheels with jobs on them that kids can do, and it made Beth feel bad spinning that wheel around and looking at all the work, because she doesn't do jobs very much. Mostly her mom does all the jobs. On Sunday Beth's mom is the busiest of all: she has to iron everybody's church clothes, and look under the bed for Beth's shoes when they're lost, and find Marnie new nylons that don't have a run, and chop up the vegetables to go with the pot roast, and make handouts for those teenagers she teaches in Sunday School ("And they don't even appreciate it!" Beth's mom says on the phone), and do lots of other things too. And Dad can't even help Mom on Sunday anymore since he's a counselor in the bishopric now and he's gone all day helping at church instead, which makes Beth's mom a little grouchy. Sometimes she gets so grouchy and so busy that she forgets Sunday is supposed to be a relaxing day. A day of rest, Beth's Primary teacher calls it.

But the good news is, right now Beth's mom is resting. A little bit after Beth and her mom and sisters got home, her mom went upstairs for a catnap—that's what she calls it—the kind of quick little nap she takes every once in a while if Dad has to stay late after church. So Beth thinks this will be the perfect time to pull out her wheel and decide what job to do.

Her wheel is very pretty. She colored it herself—purple and pink, her favorite colors—and she was very careful to stay in the lines. The wheel is fastened in the middle with a shiny gold button that lets it turn around, so Beth decides to spin it. Whatever job lands at the top, that's what she'll do. No matter if it's hard. No matter if she's never even done it before. She can do it, she knows, even if she's only in preschool and not even in kindergarten yet. Her teacher said so.

Beth closes her eyes and spins, then she opens them slowly and sees the picture at the top of the wheel: a frying pan and a chicken leg and a carrot. She can't read all the words but she knows this picture means help with dinner. She looks around the kitchen but she can't see any dinner that her mom has started, and this gives her an idea. Maybe, instead of just helping, she'll make dinner all alone. By herself. Then, after her mom wakes up she will be very *very* proud and surprised because she won't have to do any work at all.

Beth opens the fridge. At first she doesn't think there's anything inside she can cook, but then she sees a container full of beef stew way back in the corner. Beef stew is a good thing for Sundays since there's beef in it and beef is a Sunday food. Beth pulls on the container and a few things fall out of the fridge. One is some yogurt and another is a can of peaches that someone left open. Beth freezes for just a second, worried because her mom really hates spills on the floor, but she decides she can clean it up enough that her mom probably won't even notice. She goes into the guest bathroom and tugs the big blue towel down from the rack, and when she spreads it out flat on the floor she's glad to see it suck up all the sticky juice right away.

She pops the lid off the beef stew and sniffs it. She sees her mom do this a lot when she gets food from the fridge containers. It smells okay to Beth so she puts the beef stew in the microwave, with the lid off so the food can cook better. She wonders how much cooking time she should press, but she doesn't want to ask her sisters because maybe they'll try to say making dinner was all their idea. After thinking for a minute, she decides five makes sense, since Beth herself is five years old. She presses the number once on the microwave but the bowl doesn't even turn around two whole times before it stops, and she knows that's not enough cooking to make good stew. So she presses more fives, as many as the microwave will let her, and the bowl starts spinning and spinning. Soon she hears the stew hissing and popping, and when she breathes in slow she can smell the beef, warm and rich and tasty, just like it smells when Mom cooks it.

Then Beth has another good idea: She'll set the table while the stew is cooking! The glasses are high up in the cabinet—she wants the pretty glass ones, not the plastic cups her mom usually gives her—and she climbs on the counter to reach. She's very careful with the first three glasses and sets them softly on the counter by her feet, but as she's reaching for the fourth glass she forgets the other three are there and steps back. One glass crashes to the floor and Beth stands very still. She wonders if maybe nobody heard it. Maybe she can quickly jump down and sweep it up and no one will know the difference. But before she can even turn around she hears thumping on the stairs and Marnie's voice hollering, "What was that? What's going on? You better not wake up Mom!"

When Beth sees Marnie's face she starts to cry. She says, "It was an accident! An accident!" But Marnie isn't listening to her. She's running over to the microwave and she's yelling, "What are you doing? What are you thinking?" Marnie pops open the microwave door, and Beth sees the inside of the microwave, splattered all over with stew juice and meat and little pieces of carrot. The stew doesn't smell very good, anymore, either; it smells all nasty and burned, and now Beth's afraid that the fire alarm will start buzzing and wake up her mom from the catnap. She watches some stew slide from inside the microwave to the counter to the floor. It hits the ground with a soft plopping noise.

Then Tina comes downstairs with her nose wrinkled up. "What is that smell?" she says. "Gross me out!"

"Get over here and help me clean it," Marnie says, "And watch your feet because there's glass on the floor and we've got to sweep it before Mom wakes up."

Tina grabs the broom but not soon enough, because Mom already woke up. She's standing at the bottom of the stairs. Her hair is sticking out all funny from sleeping, and her makeup is under her eyes. She says, "What. Is. This." She says it just like that, stopping really long between each word. It's the way she talks when she's especially mad, so Beth is sure she's in trouble.

Both her sisters say, "Beth Did It!"

Her mom turns and looks at Beth with her eyes really big and her mouth open, and all Beth can do is cry. She's still standing on the counter but she can't get down because she's afraid of the glass on the floor. She knows her mom doesn't want her standing on the counter, though, so she starts to sit, and when she does she accidentally kicks off another nice glass. When it hits the ground with a sharp cracking sound, her mom yells, "ENOUGH!"

Beth's mom tiptoes past the glass on the floor and grabs Beth underneath her arms. She hauls her all the way up the stairs to her room without saying one word. Even though Beth is crying, "Sorry, Mommy, sorry, sorry, sorry," her mom puts her down on the bed without even looking at her. She won't even talk to her. She just closes the door behind her and leaves Beth all alone in the quiet.

Beth cries loudly for a while, hoping her mom will hear her and feel sorry and open the door and tell her she can come out, but after a few minutes she's tired and her throat hurts and she knows nobody's coming. She can hear her mom and her sisters cleaning up downstairs. She takes a shaky breath and glances around the room, wondering what to do. She's pretty sure if she got down off her bed and started playing with her toys she'd be breaking some kind of rule, so all she can do is wait. Her curtains are open, and if she tilts her head and leans a little off the side of the bed she can see outside. It's very quiet out there, and empty. No cars are driving by. No people are on the sidewalk. She decides to keep watching, though, because she hopes to see her dad's little blue truck coming down the street any minute. Her dad, for sure, will notice she's missing and come up to find her.

Then Beth hears a soft tap on the door. She wipes the tears off her face with the palms of her hands and takes a deep breath, so her mom will know she's sorry and done crying and ready to come join the rest of the family.

"Come in," Beth says.

The door opens. Marnie and Tina look in with worried faces.

"Sorry I yelled at you," Marnie says.

"Sorry I told on you," Tina says.

Beth is surprised, because usually her sisters only say sorry when their mom makes them.

"Can we hang out with you in here for a minute?" Marnie asks.

Beth nods her head. Her sisters come inside her room and close the door behind them.

They all sit cross-legged on Beth's bed. Beth worries about what she should do with them; her big sisters hardly ever come into her room because she has nothing in here but baby stuff. She knows they don't want to play Barbies, or Care Bears, and especially not Strawberry Shortcake, because Tina told her once her favorite doll, Lemon Meringue, stinks like Mom's dusting spray.

"We're thinking we'll just wait in here with you. Maybe till Dad comes home?" Tina asks.

Beth nods her head.

"We didn't want you to be up here all alone," Marnie says. "We know how it is."

They sit together for a minute without talking, listening to their mom downstairs making all her kitchen sounds: the swoosh of the refrigerator door opening and closing, the "beep, beep, beep" of the microwave timer, the clink of the dishes being set on the table.

"It was a good idea, though. Helping Mom," Marnie finally says.

"A nice idea," Tina agrees.

"Just maybe, next time, tell us too. We'll help you out." Marnie pats Beth two times on the leg.

"'Cause that's what sisters do," Tina says. "Help."

"Really?" Beth says. Because the last time she asked Marnie to help with her shoelaces, her sister made a little growling sound and said, "Maybe if you trip over them enough you'll figure it out for yourself." But when Beth looks up at her sisters, she sees their faces are serious and calm. They aren't teasing or lying or joking, she's sure.

The bedroom floor shakes just a little as the garage door rattles up. They all lean and look out the window, checking to see that it's Dad—yes, it's Dad coming home. Mom is downstairs and the kitchen is clean; dinner is coming; Dad has arrived; sisters are helpful and thoughtful and kind, sitting cross-legged right here on Beth's bed beside her. And everything is fine, now. Everything is going to be okay.

"Thanks," Beth says, and her voice is soft. She's surprised that she feels a bit shy.

"No problem," Marnie and Tina both answer, their voices chiming in together. As if they'd planned it. As if they'd always known what good sisters should say.

Nathan—1989

ભ

SUNDAY STORY #4:
ACCUSATION

Nathan hears the accusation during bishopric meeting.

"Helen Sheeney is convinced," the bishop says. "She pulled my wife aside after homemaking meeting, and once she started in, it took nearly an hour to calm her down. Helen's certain Becky Mikkelson is trying to steal her husband."

Gary, the first counselor, tilts back in his chair. A small sigh escapes his chest. "How far has it spread?"

"Not far," the bishop answers. "That's why I'm telling the both of you. Just in case you hear any rumors floating around, do your best to quiet things. Sister Mikkelson doesn't deserve to have her good name questioned based on a suspicion. And we know how Sister Sheeney can sometimes be."

Nathan, like everyone else in the Taylorsville 25th ward, knows exactly how Helen Sheeney can sometimes be. She looks innocent enough: curly-haired, partial to floral prints, so tiny it seems impossible she's borne eight children. But come to Gospel Doctrine class when Helen's in attendance and it's easy to peg her as the resident doomsayer, a whirlwind of paranoia and irrationality. When she's not reminding the ward of the coming apocalypse—for which she is fully prepared, having not one but two years' worth of food storage she will *not* be sharing with the less obedient members of the ward, as a lesson to them—she's bragging about the letter she sent to the Presiding Bishopric regarding the low-cut swimwear on display at youth conference. Among young women and their leaders alike!

"I'll keep my ear out," Gary says. "Are you going to speak to Sister Mikkelson, then?"

"I don't think that's necessary right now," the bishop says. "So far, the only evidence Sister Sheeney gave my wife is 'looks' and 'feelings' and such. So I need to talk to Helen first. Get a better handle on whether there's any merit in this at all. Hopefully, it will blow over without Sister Mikkelson even knowing about it. Does that sound all right to the two of you?"

Nathan sits silently in his chair, his palms clammy, a fist of dread in his stomach. He's been second counselor for three years now. He knows how these things work. He should speak out; he should say, "Wait, Bishop. Just hold on. Maybe Helen's not as crazy as we think she is." But he can't bring himself to say why he thinks Helen could be telling the truth. While nobody would call her husband, Peter, a great catch, he's a good guy. Polite. Easy to talk to. For years he's been the object of ward sympathy for his horrible luck in finding himself eternally hitched to Helen. Gossip has it that she was pretty good-looking as an eighteen-year-old, and didn't seem all that crazy when Peter married her. The fact that he's put up with her this long is seen as a testament to his being a stand-up guy—exactly the kind of man Becky Mikkelson wishes she had for herself. Nathan knows this from personal experience.

The first time Becky came on to him, Nathan wasn't sure how to take it. Becky and Nathan's wife, Alicia, went way back. She was one of Alicia's first good friends when they moved into the ward, and

Nathan had always been cordial to her. Friendly. She was an undeniably pretty woman: tall, curvy, blessed with a wide, willing smile and bright eyes. Nathan was self-consciously careful never to give her too much attention, a reflexive fear of the appearance of impropriety that went all the way back to his mission days. Not that Nathan had any reason to let his eye wander, of course. His wife Alicia was beautiful as well—almost forty and she could still fit into her size-six jeans from high school—but a man could never be too careful.

Nathan and Alicia double-dated with Becky and her husband, Tom, only once. Nathan never really considered Tom his kind of guy. Everything about him was clipped and severe, from his imperious voice to his meticulous hairstyle. Alicia didn't like him, either, calling him a jerk and a male chauvinist. Nathan was stunned to learn that he had yet to change a diaper, after fathering four children in eight years. Alicia often wondered aloud how her friend put up with him, especially since Becky "didn't take crap from anybody else, ever."

But one way or another, they got wrangled into this double date. They went to see some spy thriller—a James Bond, maybe? Nathan couldn't remember—but it was the way Tom treated Becky at dinner afterward that Nathan would never forget. They went to the Old Spaghetti Factory, and not only did Tom interrupt Becky almost every time she opened her mouth, but he confiscated her complementary spumoni ice cream. Literally snatched it away from her the minute the waiter turned his back.

"We both know who doesn't need this," he said. Nathan remembers how Tom tried to keep his tone light and playful—as if his comment were part of some hilarious marital game the two of them regularly played—but it didn't work. He sounded cutting and cruel. Almost scary.

"Whatever, Tom." Becky rolled her eyes in Alicia's direction. Alicia pursed her lips.

After that, the conversation was uncomfortable and stilted, and the night ended early. Nathan and Alicia came home to an empty house—their girls were spending the evening at his mom's place, and she wasn't due to bring them back for another couple of hours. Alicia took the opportunity to run to the store and get some groceries. Nathan sat down and flicked on the TV. Moments later, he heard a soft knock at the door.

Becky stood on the front porch. She looked a mess. Her eyes were red and puffy, and she'd cried off all her makeup. Her face and neck were mottled pink.

"Oh, for Pete's sake," she said. She wiped her runny nose on her sleeve. "Just my luck that Alicia doesn't answer. Ha!" She tried to laugh.

Nathan wasn't sure what to say, so he apologized. "Sorry," he said, a little embarrassed for both of them.

"Oh, no," Becky said, waving her hands in front of her face. "I can't believe I just said that. I didn't mean it that way. I mean, against you. I'm just such a wreck. I hate having anybody see me like this."

"Don't worry about me," Nathan said. "Don't worry about what I think. Really. You're fine."

"I'm fine. Oh yes! Fine, fine, fine." She sang out the final sentence in a frantic soprano that made Nathan nervous.

"Alicia's not here, though. Right now. Sorry." He tried to sound sympathetic.

Becky sighed and leaned her head against the doorframe. She took a deep, shuddering breath. "Of course," she whispered. "Of course she's not."

"But I'll tell her . . ."

She interrupted before he could finish. "I mean, I shouldn't have to take it anymore. I shouldn't!" Her head remained bowed against the doorframe, obscuring her face, but Nathan could see her shoulders heaving as she began to cry in earnest.

Nathan wasn't sure what to do. Here Becky was, a woman in real distress, standing at his door and sobbing and making no move to leave. Would Alicia understand if he invited her in, he wondered? What would she think if she came home and found the two of them alone in the house? But how could he send Becky away in such a state?

"Do you need to come inside?" he offered.

She immediately nodded and sniffed and shuffled inside. She headed straight for the living room and curled up in the corner of the couch like a teenager, hugging her knees with her arms, her legs tucked in.

She lifted her eyes to Nathan as he stood in the entry. He kept his hands in his pockets.

"Tom is a terrible husband, you know," she said. "He yells at me. Yells at the kids. Tells me I'm fat."

Her face was pleading, naked with emotion. It felt ridiculous to Nathan to be standing so far away from her—twenty feet? thirty?—when she obviously needed consoling. The last thing he should be conveying to her was more rejection. Yet he didn't know how he should respond. And what should he say? She wasn't fat—far from it. More voluptuous, really, but he couldn't say *that* to a woman who wasn't his wife.

She continued looking up at him, her eyebrows raised, expectant.

He walked toward her and sat down gingerly on the edge of the couch. "He shouldn't say that," he said softly. He hoped this response would do the trick, make her take a deep breath and sit up straight, but instead she covered her face with her hands. Soon the sound of choking sobs escaped through her splayed fingers.

"Hey," he said. "Hey, now." He reached out a hand to touch her sympathetically on the shoulder, but then he remembered himself and pulled away before he made contact.

Becky's head was down, she didn't see. "I'm such a mess," she moaned. She reached over and grabbed a tissue from the end table and blew her nose, then looked up and smiled sadly.

"No. No you're not," Nathan said. Even though, obviously, she was. But she wasn't always a mess. Usually she looked great. Just not right now. "You're not a mess at all. Don't say things like that about yourself. Don't use that negative talk."

73

"You think that's negative talk? You should listen to Tom. He could teach you a thing or two about negative talk."

Tom. It was guys like him who gave men a bad name, Nathan thought. And a good woman like Becky—actually, any woman, when you think about it—didn't deserve his kind of treatment.

"It's not right that he should treat you like that. I mean it. Negative stuff, there's no place for it in a marriage. You've got to stay positive, build each other up. It's the only way."

"I know!" Becky exclaimed. "Exactly! That's exactly what I tell him. But does he listen to me? Ever? No."

"Well he should. You deserve it."

"I do deserve it." She looked up at Nathan, suddenly full of conviction. "You're totally right. I deserve a lot of things, you know. I'm a good wife."

"I'm sure you are," Nathan agreed. He noticed her shoulders losing tension and a more even color coming into her cheeks. He could see her countenance changing, brightening and relaxing, and a flash of satisfaction charged through him. He was doing it, he thought. He was helping.

"And I'm not going to take his crap any more," Becky said.

"And you shouldn't. Never again!" He raised his fist in the air and shook it, smiling.

Becky looked at him fondly, her eyes still misty with tears. "Alicia's so lucky."

Nathan slowly lowered his fist. "She is?"

"She is. She's got a guy like you. She doesn't even know how lucky she is."

Becky placed her hand on his leg, just above his knee, and squeezed. Nathan drew in one sharp breath.

"If I had a husband like you, I'd appreciate you." She looked at him earnestly, not moving her hand.

"Well. Yes. I don't know." He turned his face away from her, simultaneously flattered and terrified, his heart thumping loudly against his ribcage.

"You've helped me so much, Nathan. Just in these few minutes. You've said more nice things to me just now than Tom has said in, I don't know. Years. You can't even realize." Then, before he knew what was happening, she gathered him up in an embrace. She held him tight, her warm breath tickling his neck. He leaned into her for one brief moment and felt how soft she was, soft and sad and undeserving of all the pain her husband was causing. Then she released him from her grip and the realization of who he was—a married man, alone in his house with a vulnerable woman—rushed in and filled his chest with an uncomfortable tightness. He pulled back, flushed and blinking.

"I'm sorry," she said. "I get wound up like this and I just go on . . ."

Nathan stood up quickly. Could she see the panic on his face, he wondered? Could she tell? "No, no, don't you worry. You're fine. Everything's fine. I'll tell Alicia you came, okay?" He could hear the tenor of his voice. Strained. Unnerved. He concentrated on his face, rearranging his expression to one of calm neutrality.

Becky stood. She ran her fingers through her hair and took a deep breath. "I know I'm emotional. Crazy. This whole night has just been crazy!" She smiled. "But I needed someone to talk to or else I just might have exploded. And you were the perfect guy to talk to. The perfect one."

"Oh, no, no. Anybody would have . . ." He let the sentence trail away. He walked to the front door and opened it.

"I mean it." She stood beside him in the doorway. "You're the best."

"I don't know about that." Nathan gave a little laugh, staccato and unconvincing, then turned to look down the street. Alicia's car wasn't coming. "Like I said, I'll tell Alicia you came by."

"Sure," she said. "But you can tell her I'm okay now. After talking to you, I'm really okay." She walked out to her car, but before Nathan had a chance to close the front door, she turned and looked up at him one last time. She smiled. Her eyes were teary and bright.

"Thank you," she mouthed. She raised her hand and waved.

75

Nathan closed the door quickly. It wasn't until she was safely away from him and down the street that he realized he'd forgotten to wave back.

After that day, he avoided Becky as best he could. But she and Alicia were friends, they were in the same ward, and after a little time passed Nathan convinced himself he'd misread her signals. Becky was a good person—maybe a bit lonely, and married to a jerk—but not the type to make an intentional pass at the husband of one of her best friends. A few years went by without another incident, and Nathan had almost put the significance of that day out of his mind until the ward Christmas party. Nathan had stayed late to help the shorthanded activities committee clean up. He knew she was on the committee; still, he was surprised when she popped her head into the Primary room, where he was cleaning up all alone.

"Hey," she said. "You need help?"

He did. The room was a mess: candy cane wrappers on the floor, chairs strewn everywhere, sprinkles from the Christmas cookies ground into the carpet. He paused for a moment, feeling a brief pang of concern. But why should he be concerned, really? If he couldn't trust himself, who could he trust? "Sure," he said. "The quicker this goes, the quicker we're out of here."

"Well, I'm a good little worker bee," she said, and climbed on a chair and began pulling down the crepe paper attached to the ceiling. He looked up because he was concerned for her safety. The chair was rickety—he'd seen it wobble—and he wanted to make sure she wouldn't fall. But he let his eyes linger a fraction of a second too long as she lifted her arms over her head and stretched her body to reach the decorations, and she caught him. Like any woman used to being looked at, she could feel it, even with her back to him. She turned and glanced over her shoulder, a hint of a smile playing on her lips.

"So, you going to work or what?" she asked, her voice a little breathy. Flirtatious. Her eyes flashed vivid blue.

Nathan looked away. "I'm getting right to it," he said, a bit too cheerfully.

They worked in silence for a moment, then Becky said, "I still think about that day you comforted me, you know."

"What was that?" Nathan kept moving, folding up and stacking chairs.

"You know what I'm talking about." She hopped off her chair and walked over to where Nathan was working. She leaned casually against the wall. "I know you remember."

Nathan didn't answer.

"Sometimes I think about it when things are bad between Tom and me. How kind you were. And then I think about Alicia and how she complains and I just get . . ."

Nathan stopped working. He met Becky's gaze, curious now. "She complains?"

"Oh, you know. Little things. Petty things. Drives me crazy, though. Here you are, such a nice guy, good to her, and handsome . . ."

Nathan felt his pulse accelerate.

"You are!" she laughed. "You're the kind of man I should have picked, if I'd only known better."

"Come on," he said. He knew, now, he should stop the conversation. Politely excuse himself and leave. But Becky's bright eyes, her open smile, even her way of standing with her shoulders thrust back and her arms hanging loose at her sides seemed so easy and nonthreatening at that moment. Inviting.

"Do you ever have those thoughts?" she asked. "Like if I had it to do all over again, I would have done it differently? I could have made my life happier?"

In a flash, Nathan imagined a life with Becky: her easy laugh, her attentiveness. For just a moment he even thought about her body, so full and yielding, completely different from Alicia's. Alicia. Her name snapped his mind back into focus.

"Becky, we shouldn't be talking this way."

A flicker of irritation moved across Becky's face. "Why? Why not?"

"Just, we shouldn't. I don't think. It just seems . . ." he paused, searching for the word.

"Inappropriate?"

"Yes! That's it. Inappropriate."

"Fine. We'll work then." She grabbed up an armful of chairs and dragged them across the room. She didn't even try to stack them neatly, letting the chairs fall against each other in uneven rows, the clang of metal on metal ringing through the room.

"Becky?" Nathan offered, afraid he'd hurt her feelings, hoping if he appeared conciliatory she'd stop making such a racket.

"I'm just so *sick* of that word," she said, her voice tight with anger. "'Inappropriate.' I'm not doing anything wrong. Neither are you. We're talking—*talking*—and that's somehow against the rules? I get so tired of tiptoeing around everybody all the time. Especially men." She pointed her manicured finger at Nathan. "A woman should be able to talk to a man. I mean, are men that weak? I can't even mention that I think Alicia should treat you better without you turning it into some kind of sexual thing?"

Nathan stiffened. "I never said it was a sexual thing."

"Then why shouldn't we be talking this way?" She folded her arms across her chest. She stared at him, bold, unflinching. "You tell me."

He shifted his eyes away from Becky's face. It was late. Soon Alicia would be missing him.

Becky sighed. "Like I would even try, anyway. Like I don't know how much you love your wife."

"And I do love her."

"That's all I was trying to say. That she's lucky and doesn't even know to appreciate it." She put her hand on the knob of the closed door beside her. Then she smiled. "And don't worry. I won't tell."

After the bishopric meeting and all during Sacrament, Nathan thinks about his responsibilities: to Helen, to the bishop. To Becky. To the truth. The minute the bishop started telling Helen's story, Nathan knew the accusation had some validity to it. It probably hasn't gotten to the point of outright adultery—Peter is a good man, and Nathan doubts if Becky, even, would go that far—but he also knows Becky and how desperate she is. Alicia tells him that her marriage to Tom is only getting worse. And it isn't fair to Peter, having to fend off advances from such a beautiful, needy woman. The poor guy's married to Helen, for heaven's sake. Catch both Peter and Becky on an especially weak day, and who knows what could happen?

He decides that instead of going to Sunday School, he'll take a detour past the Primary room and try to find Becky, hopefully alone. She was recently called to be the Primary president and she's often out in the hall, rummaging through her closets, making sure the Primary runs like clockwork.

The hall is empty. He walks over to the Primary room, pokes his head in, and sees Becky in front of the children, reading a story from the *Friend*. She is a good storyteller. Even though she's reading from a magazine, she has all the children in the room quiet, listening attentively. She's an excellent Primary president, so good the bishop often says he doesn't know what he'd do without her. She looks up from her magazine and sees Nathan. Without missing a word in her narrative, she raises one finger to indicate she'll be right out to speak with him. Nathan nods his head and retreats to the hall.

He becomes more and more nervous as he waits. He scans up and down the empty hall, hoping—praying—that the bishop or Alicia doesn't stumble upon him and ask what he's up to. He's never been a good liar. They would see right through him immediately.

Finally Becky bursts out of the Primary room. Her cheeks are red and she seems a little breathless, almost winded, and he wonders how a person can get herself so worked up reading a story to a bunch of kids.

"Official business?" she asks.

It's been two years since that Christmas, two years since Nathan has talked to her in any capacity other than as a courteous fellow ward member—or as second counselor. She probably assumes he's here at the request of the bishop.

"Not really," Nathan says. He runs his hand through his hair. "Well, kind of. Maybe."

"So is it or isn't it?" Becky says lightly. "Fess up! Are you guys in the bishopric letting the Relief Society steal my music leader or something?"

"Not quite." Nathan takes a deep breath. "I just have to ask you a favor."

"All right."

Nathan looks over his shoulder. Two kids have escaped from Sunday School and are messing around near the back door, pushing each other into the coat hangers. The sound of jangling metal ricochets down the hall.

"Hey, guys," Nathan yells. The boys glance at him sullenly, then shuffle away.

"There's got to be a way to keep those kids in class," Becky says. "I hear bribing them with candy sometimes works." She's smiling, completely unaware.

Now the hall is empty. This is the time to say what must be said. Move on. Be done. He leans in. Becky follows his lead and leans in too, her brow creased with curiosity.

"I'm going to have to ask that you stay away from Peter Sheeney," Nathan says softly.

Becky blinks and ticks her head to the side. "Meaning?" She is whispering as well.

"You need to stay away from Peter Sheeney. Helen's been talking. She has some—what should I call them?—some, um, concerns." Nathan can feel the sweat starting along his hairline. His lungs constrict inside his chest and he's afraid she can hear his quick breathing.

"She's got *concerns?*" Becky backs up. "You can't be serious."

"Don't worry, though. The bishop and Gary don't believe her." Nathan realizes he's looking down at the floor and quickly glances up to read her expression, but she doesn't seem worried at all. In fact, she's twisted her mouth into a smirk. The look of disdain reminds him of his daughter Tina, who is thirteen years old and never sorry. Never wrong.

Becky gives a derisive snort. "I'll have you know I've probably spoken to Peter all of five or six times in my entire life." Her voice has returned to its normal volume.

Nathan gathers up his courage. "But given our past history, you know . . ."

A slow smile spreads across Becky's face. "So that's what this is all about."

"No, no. It's not. Trust me! This isn't about me. It's about Peter. And Helen. And you."

"Right," she says slowly. "Well, Peter's a friendly acquaintance. Nothing more."

"Like I was a friendly acquaintance?"

"Oh, geez." Becky rolls her eyes. "Don't flatter yourself."

Now Nathan is upset. He was there. He knows what happened. She came on to him, not once, but twice. She understands her power over men like him—men like Peter, too—and she uses it. Gets a kind of charge from it. And she can't pretend she doesn't.

"I'm only saying that Peter is probably vulnerable to your advances." Nathan realizes his own voice has increased in volume. He scans up and down the hallway, relieved to find no one within earshot. "It's dangerous, is all," he whispers. "You're walking a thin line."

Becky tilts toward Nathan, as near to him as she's been in years. Her face is just inches from his. Her breath smells like peppermint.

"What are you," she whispers. "Jealous?"

Nathan's mouth falls open. "What? You've got to be kidding me. What?"

"You accuse me, I accuse you. It's only fair."

"I haven't done anything wrong," Nathan says. "Not a thing."

"And neither have I." She pulls her shoulders back and stands up straight. With her heels on, she's a very tall woman. Her eyes are burning and her cheeks blaze pink. "Remember that."

After church, the bishop pulls Nathan into his office.

"I spoke with Sister Sheeney," he says. "Helen agrees now that she was overreacting. Just so you know. So you don't think anything, well, unjustified about Sister Mikkelson."

"Oh, of course not," Nathan says. "Of course I don't."

"Nothing worse than having crazy rumors flying!" The bishop claps Nathan on the back. "But if you hear any talk going around, make sure you put the rumors to rest. If you hear anything from your wife, or anyone."

"Definitely, I will."

"Good, good. Glad to see this episode pass."

The ward clerk taps on the door, and the bishop excuses himself. Church is over and Nathan is ready to go home. He leaves the office, eager to search for his family in the halls. He wants to find them fast, get home, have dinner. Put this day behind him.

Nathan scans the foyer. He can't find his family, but he sees Becky across the room, her husband standing beside her, his hand at the small of her back. She turns her head and sees Nathan looking, and she holds his gaze, unafraid. Nathan is the first to look away.

Alicia—1992

⋐ℬ

MOTHER ANGEL

When I can't sleep I often think of you, Mother. When it's dark, silent, still. When the clouds are whispering by. Some nights I slide out of bed and go to my window and imagine your spirit mingling with the heavy air, swirling in the breeze, and I wonder if you pass me by and see my face looking out into the night, and if you know my thoughts, that they're of you.

What do I think of you? This mother that I've never known. You are the girl in the black-and-white photographs, your dark hair spilling past your shoulders, slash of lipstick bold against the whiteness of your face. I've never seen your colors. Your eyes, green or hazel? Your skin, olive or milky or tinged with pink? In the pictures there are only whites and blacks and shades of gray, your head tilted this way or that, your eyes full of secrets. I do know you were beautiful. Even without the pictures I would know it. Dad tells me, Grandma Louise, your brother, Uncle Steven. "How beautiful she was!" They sigh it, as if your beauty makes your loss that much more painful to a daughter. "Your mother. So beautiful, and so young."

Twenty-one years old. Can someone who died at twenty-one even be my mother anymore? I want to ask you: have you stayed that age, or are you whirling around the spirit world as a thirty-year-old, the age I've heard some speculate in Sunday School we will be throughout eternity, our bodies held forever in perfect maturity? I am forty-two. When I die and come rushing out of the light and meet you, finally, maybe I will be the elderly one, bent and frail, and you will still be young and crisp as a photograph, unwrinkled, perfectly preserved. But we will know each other. We will remember. For twenty-seven hours you knew me, held me, studied my face. Perhaps my eyes were the last thing you ever saw in this life: the gaze of the child you gave your life for, who left you bleeding yourself pale.

On Memorial Day I take my girls to visit you. The wind is always whipping: American flags waving frantically, vases blowing over, old women losing their hats. Sometimes the girls complain. They stand holding their hair back with their hands, and they say, "Hurry, Mom! Let's go!" And it's hard to justify lingering because, after all, I never knew you. But my secret is I like the wind. In my mind it's all the spirits come to visit, dashing from family to family, checking to see that they've been remembered. I want to stay there long enough that you can find me.

Have you found me? Or did you move on, long ago? When I was a child, I believed you were with me always, watching, approving or disapproving, nudging me in one direction or the other. In certain moments, the thought of your involvement in my life comforted me—but it also left me confused, and even sad. For years, people told me it was you who sent Jean to Dad to ease his loneliness, and to give me a family to join. How I hated those people when I was a girl! Jean and her boys were bad enough, but to think it was your doing? I didn't want to believe it. But I wondered: if it were in a spirit's power to send somebody, wouldn't it be in a spirit's power to *stop* someone from coming? Maybe you could have mustered the powers of heaven to open Dad's eyes, to help him see all the pain in his only daughter's future and prevent him from marrying again. But you didn't. When I got older I decided it wasn't possible; I grew to believe spirits were impotent observers, watching their loved ones drawn along the paths of their own particular fates. It was easier for me to love you, after that.

And I don't hate her anymore. Jean. I think I understand, now, why she rejected me. All those people saying, "Alicia! The perfect picture of her mother!" She knew Dad could see you in me, and he would always love that perfect picture best. Now she's dead too. Have you met her yet? Since the spirit world is not quite heaven, it seems to me the capacity for anger—or revenge—could still remain, and I don't want you to spend too much time thinking it's your job to get back at her for me. Or maybe I'm wrong. Maybe everything up there is all peace and love, and when you saw her you embraced her, completely forgiven. Maybe it was easier to do because she has no claim on Dad—or you, or me—because she was a widow when she married him, sealed already in the temple to her dead husband Max. Max the benevolent. Max the wise. I remember the pictures she kept of him around the house for her boys. So they wouldn't forget, she said. He looked so pompous and bored, his jowls hanging down like a bulldog's, his eyes all baggy and tired, and I felt bad for her boys, then. That this was their dad—for eternity! No getting around it!—and I got to keep my dad, and beautiful you. Those times, I remembered to feel lucky.

How ironic, then, that my own girls don't feel fortunate. They don't understand what a blessing it is to live in a house where we all belong to each other. Sometimes I tell them, "You kids don't know how good you've got it." When I say it they avoid my eyes. I think they're afraid I'll see the truth in their faces: that having a real mother —a woman who confiscates their blue mascara, makes them scrub out the toilet for money, who tells them their skirts are too short and their grades are too poor and their music's too loud and "If you think you're getting away with this one you've got another thing coming!" —maybe this real mother will always come in a distant second to the imaginary kind. The benevolent angel mother, eternally patient, eternally kind, who, if she had lived, would most certainly have loved her child perfectly.

I am not a perfect mother. I make mistakes. Tina will tell you. Tonight she screamed at me. "I Hate You!" she shrieked, and slammed her bedroom door in my face. It all started because of Keith, this horrible skateboarding boy with his baggy pants and disdainful smirk, thinking he can slouch around our house and treat me like some kind of intruder when she's *my* daughter. It's *my* choice, still, to decide with whom she spends her time, and how, and when. Tonight I kicked him out. I came downstairs and the two of them were in the kitchen eating the brownies I'd made for the Young Women's activity and I lost it. "Out!" I told him, and pointed my finger at the door. I didn't even explain. I just said, "Out, now." I could see Tina looking at me, incredulous, then she said, "Wait, Mom, what are you doing? Why are you mad at us?" Do you know what I said to her? "Like you care about anyone but yourself. Get out of my sight." I said that. Yelled it. "Get out of my sight." Then her face fell in, and she ran up to her room.

I sat in the kitchen for a while thinking about what I'd done and why. If Marnie had brought a boy to the house and they'd done something as innocent as eating a few brownies that weren't meant for them, would I have kicked the boy out of the house, would I have yelled at her, called her selfish, ordered her to leave my sight? No. Never. But Marnie wouldn't have brought a boy like Keith into my house in the first place. She wouldn't have looked up at me with that willful kind of challenge in her eye, that *hardness*, that Tina has mastered so well. She loves the fact I don't like Keith, I don't like her clothes or her music or her friends. It makes her happy to wave a cheerful good-bye to Marnie and me as we head out to Mutual without her. Which was another reason I was angry—the brownies were for the young women who actually *go* to Mutual, and I'd considered using them as a pathetic little bribe to see if she'd come.

But I felt sick, like I always do after one of our confrontations. She's drowning, my Tina, but whenever I extend my hand to try and pull her to safety, she slaps it away, and her willfulness makes me so angry I can't help myself. I nudge her right back and she ends up even farther away, in deeper water. Soon I won't be able to reach her at all.

I went up to her room to apologize. I knocked, but her music was screaming and howling—painful music, angry music—and I knew she couldn't hear me. I balled up my fist and I pounded. Nothing. So I opened the door. She saw me and her face gathered together with rage, her eyes shrinking narrow and hard, her mouth tight. She pulled herself up tall and strode to the door so she was standing just an inch from my face. Then she screamed. "I Hate You!" She shrieked it, as loud as she could, and her words hit me like a physical force. It was as if her rage and her hatred had taken root and grown inside her to something palpable, something she could hurl at me, and I felt my body take it: hot breath, spray of spit, fury. She slammed the door and I couldn't move. *Who is this girl?* I thought. *What have I created?*

How do I be a mother? I don't know. You never taught me. You left me to myself. To Jean. Do you know she never even did my hair? "I'm no one to muddle around with girl things," she told me. I see photos of myself at seven, eight, nine years old, and I wonder, *Who was taking care of this child?* In my elementary school pictures, standing with my class on the auditorium steps, I look rumpled and forgotten. In one of them I'm standing next to Evelyn Bradstreet, a girl I hated and adored because she was so beautiful. Every day she came to school with her hair in two long braids tied up with colored ribbons, the part in the middle as sharp and straight as a furrow in a corn field, and I imagined how much that girl's mother must love her, to be so meticulous. So careful. One day I told Jean that I wanted my hair like Evelyn's and do you know what she did? She took out the clippers, the ones she used on her boys the first Saturday of every month to keep their buzz cuts neat, and she flicked it on and held it under my chin. "This is my kind of hairdressing," she said, the clippers humming in her hand. When I ran away, crying, to my room she said, "Come on, now. Can't you take a joke?" Dad wasn't home. These were the things she did when he wasn't watching.

I wonder if you saw it; if you were there, angry for me and unable to intervene. Or maybe you're here right now. It's possible you're right behind me. Your hand—it's on my shoulder. Your breath is warm against my neck.

"Don't worry," you want to tell me. "Everything turns out fine in the end."

Are you sure? I want to believe you. You are my mother and these are the things that mothers tell their children. Their daughters, especially.

"I see things that you can't see," you tell me. "Trust me! The world is very clear and very bright, and the future isn't difficult to find."

I close my eyes. Even in the darkness I can see light moving behind my lids, slow, fluid, easy. I imagine you moving like the light. Around me, above me. Calm.

I want to trust you. I do.

Marnie—1993–1996

 C3

TRYING

Home for Thanksgiving during her sophomore year of college, Marnie listened to her mother complain.

"I've told your sister," her mother said. "Six months to graduation. Don't get pregnant. Don't get arrested. Then you can be on your way."

Marnie and her mother stood side-by-side, drying the good silver that sat in piles next to the sink. With dinner over and the relatives gone, her mother felt comfortable telling Marnie all the Tina stories: the broken promises, the stubborn rebellions, the selfishness. Tina was a senior in high school now, tall and bright with anger. She'd made only one appearance on Thanksgiving Day, during dessert, and Marnie noticed the way she carved herself through the clusters of chatting relatives with her elbows out, unapologetic. She dared them all to look her in the face.

Marnie was not afraid of her. This, after all, was her sister, only twenty months behind her, and up until the last few years the whole of their lives had been lived as if it were the same life: same toys shared, same socks worn, same bedtimes kept, same jokes remembered. They used to press their hands together and measure the length of their fingers, and even though Marnie was older, their hands were always exactly the same size.

"I'll talk to her," Marnie said.

"You don't have to do that," her mother replied. "It's not your problem."

"Somebody needs to talk to her besides you or Dad. We're sisters. Maybe I can get through to her."

When Tina breezily announced she was heading to a party later that day, Marnie was surprised by her parents' acquiescence. Tina simply grabbed her keys off the kitchen counter and said, "I'll be home sometime tonight," and nobody made a peep. Her father didn't say, *You get back here, young lady. Thanksgiving is a family day.* He didn't ask, *But where is this party, anyway?* Her mother didn't even glance over in Tina's direction. They seemed too weary. Beaten into submission.

So that night Marnie went to bed in Tina's room. She tucked herself under her sister's quilt and waited. The night was long and she had a lot of time to prepare what she should say. She closed her eyes and prayed, asking Heavenly Father to give her the words to help change her sister's life, and alone there, in the silence, she could have sworn the air felt thicker. Heavier, somehow, with inspiration. She felt strong and brave, ready to fight the good fight, eager to make a difference.

At a little after two in the morning Tina swung herself into the room. She smelled of smoke and sweat, and her mascara had run from one eye down to the middle of her cheek. She stopped short in the doorway and made a sound at her sister, like a snort and a sigh, and suddenly Marnie felt ridiculous sitting there in her flannel pajamas with the scriptures balanced on her knees.

Marnie opened the scriptures and said to her sister, "I've found something I want to read to you, because I love you and I'm afraid for you, how you're wasting your life, how you're forgetting everything we ever learned. It's about repentance."

Marnie started to read, but her voice sounded hollow and anxious.

She noticed Tina looking up at the ceiling, her arms crossed tightly at her chest. She began to wonder if perhaps this was a bad idea. The timing was off, or the place was all wrong, or she didn't understand what it felt like to come home late from a party buzzed and exhausted, wanting to fall into bed. Not wanting to talk to your sister about self-worth and true joy and God. But she'd made a commitment. She had to see it through.

Marnie had four scriptures to share with her sister and she read each one straight through. When she finished she sniffed, clapped the Book of Mormon closed, lifted her eyebrows and met her sister's gaze. They stayed like that, eyes locked together, for a few long seconds.

Finally Tina spoke. "Answer me this," she said slowly, intent on Marnie's face. "How can you even stand yourself?"

A good question, Marnie thought. And one she couldn't answer.

After Thanksgiving break Marnie returned to BYU. For years she'd heard stories about people "finding themselves" in college, how breaking away from one's family allowed a person's true identity to emerge. She waited for this emergence—for her authentic self to wriggle free like a butterfly from a chrysalis—but semester after semester passed by, and nothing seemed to happen. She spent a lot of time thinking about herself and whether she was a problem to people—all her earnestness, all her trying—but she wasn't sure how to go about changing things. Boys liked her, but the wrong boys: dutiful, solemn, wife-seeking boys who liked feeling righteous when they opened her car door. She got a sense that her girlfriends respected her more than they loved her. "You make me want to be better, to do better," her roommate told her, before bolting out the door and heading to a party to which Marnie had not been invited.

During her final two years at school, Marnie found herself watching people on campus, girls in particular, loud and beautiful girls specifically. The way their limbs moved, loose and easy. The way they never seemed in a hurry. As she watched them she knew she could never be one of them, but she also recognized a certain joy these girls had learned that she must be entitled to as well.

Her parents and her grandma and her little sister Beth came to Provo for her graduation. Not only had she gotten her B.A. in history and her secondary teaching certificate in record time, but in her family she was the first to graduate from anywhere magna cum laude. Yet, sitting in her seat among the graduates, she was overcome by the smell of perfume and hairspray, the whispering and bumping, all the frenzied waving. In their blue gowns, shoulder-to-shoulder, they all appeared to be the same person when seen from a distance, she was sure. *Who are my parents watching?* she wondered. *How can they even find me?*

The girls on either side of her both sported fat diamond rings on their left hands. In front of her, two skinny blondes with identical spiral perms discussed their mission calls in loud whispers. Marnie concentrated on her own deep breathing. She should have been one of these girls, she knew. It was the logical progression: college graduation, no ring, mission call. She'd spent many nights praying, some nights crying, even, but she couldn't will herself to want to spend the next year and a half with either of these curly-haired girls, struggling to learn Spanish or Thai, shuffling along dusty streets in low-heeled shoes. And to make matters even worse, the thought of starting her career, spending her days discussing the Revolutionary War with seventh graders, filled her with fear and regret.

After two hours, the dean finally called her name. She strode solemnly across the stage. She thought she heard her father's lone voice—"Woo-hoo!"—echoing around the auditorium. She kept her gaze fixed straight ahead. She saw her destiny, thin and tight as a guitar string. She wondered if she should cut her hair.

Of all the sisters, Marnie was the only one to keep her hair long through junior high and onward. When they were children, their mother had been famous for the intricate and original hairstyles she practiced on each of her three daughters: French twists, complicated braids, enormous starchy bows and beaded barrettes. No sister's hair had been more than briskly trimmed all through grade school. Both of Marnie's younger sisters had demanded the newest hairstyle or perm before turning twelve, but Marnie had always been too proud of her hair to cut it. She would brush it to a gleam and let it hang down the length of her back, dark and shiny as a cat's. People noticed it. Strangers, even, would sometimes comment. But beyond the look of her hair, Marnie had viewed its length as a sign of perseverance. An emblem of her ability to set goals and see them through.

Now two weeks had passed since graduation, and Marnie wasn't washing her hair much. She was living at her parents' house, going to bed early and waking up late, watching game shows and listening to her mother talk on the phone. Sometimes her mother went into the laundry room to talk, ostensibly to keep her daughter from overhearing, but Marnie would mute the television and hear phrases like "driving me crazy with her sighing and wandering around" coming at her from under the door.

Midway into week three her parents sat her down at the dining room table. It was clear she wasn't calling school districts or sending out her résumé and no mention had been made of preparing missionary papers.

"What's the plan?" her mother asked.

"We only want to help," her father said.

She thought about Tina, living far away now in California with a boy named Jimmy, and the life she must have: unencumbered by expectations, free from questions.

"I don't know what to tell you." Marnie traced a gouge in the table with her fingernail. The motorized hum of the refrigerator cycled off, enveloping the room in silence.

"So that's it?" her mother finally asked. "We're done here?"

"If I knew what to tell you, I would say it," Marnie said. "I'll let you know when I come up with something."

Her mother opened her mouth like a fish. She turned her face to Marnie's father.

"So this is what we're getting from *her* now? We're getting sarcasm now?"

Marnie laughed, two sharp staccato notes. She couldn't help herself. It came to her that, in her entire adolescence, she'd never had a conversation like this with either of her parents. Now here she sat, slump-shouldered and sullen at twenty-one. She supposed it would be fitting to huff up to her room, fling herself on the bed, and turn up the volume on her stereo. Instead she looked her mother in the eye.

"It's not sarcasm," she said. "I'm telling you the truth. And now I'd like to go to bed."

She concentrated on walking up the stairs calmly, like an adult. No trudging or clomping. After closing the bedroom door behind her, she could hear her mother pushing in the dining room chairs hard and fast, the scrape of the legs a shrill squeak against the hardwood floor.

She woke the next morning before dawn. For the first time in weeks she had a plan. She took the scissors from her mother's craft closet, situated herself in the guest bathroom with a towel across her shoulders, and wet her hair down with a spray bottle. She gathered her hair in the circle of her palm and started cutting. Her right hand trembled as the scissors pushed through the coarse thickness of it, but finally the hair broke free and fell into the basin of the sink. It curled into itself like a dead animal. She wondered if she should leave it there for her mother to find.

She kept cutting, watching as loose hairs floated down past her shoulders and onto the floor. Her head and neck felt loose and light. Her blood raced under her skin, thrilled and terrified.

When she finished cutting, she raised her eyes to the mirror, held in all her breath, and looked. Her hair hung jagged across her collar, the ends choppy and uneven. An empty-eyed stranger gazed back at her. A girl with a pale and doughy neck, a jutting chin. She saw the face of a crazy person, a lost and lonely person, a person she had never met.

She looked at her hand holding the scissors and at the mess, the terrible chaotic mess of her own wet hair clumped on the floor, strays clinging to the wall and sink and toilet. It looked to Marnie like the scene of a violent, passionate crime.

It took her fifteen minutes to clean everything up. Through the window, she could see light from the rising sun edging along the mountains. Her heart sped in panic that she might be found there on her hands and knees, scrubbing the floor, her hair piled up in the sink without excuse or explanation. But she was fast and thorough. She checked every crevice, caught every hair, wrapped it all up tight in a towel and threw it in the garbage can in the garage. She left the bathroom spotless, as if no one had been there at all.

She crept upstairs to her bedroom where she waited in the gray morning light until she heard the family stirring. She buried herself in her bedspread, the covers up around her neck and ears. After she heard the door slam for the final time, she let the stillness settle until she could be absolutely sure she was alone. Then she put on her shoes and drove herself to Great Clips, where a silent woman named Sandy gave her a tidy new bob.

Within a week Marnie found a receptionist job at a mortgage company and a cheap apartment in Cedar City, a college town four hours south of home. On move-in day her father helped her unload the tiny U-Haul trailer. Her mother scrubbed out her bathtub and laid contact paper in all the kitchen cupboards. Marnie bought herself a table and chairs on clearance at K-Mart and hung yellow curtains in the bedroom.

After she settled in, her mother made a point of calling every night to pass on neighborhood news and discuss the ridiculousness of Marnie's move. "I don't know what you think you'll find in Cedar

City," she said. Or, "The least you could do is apply to a graduate program."

Girls Marnie knew started leaving on missions: a high school friend went to New Jersy, a couple of girls from her home ward went to South America, one terrified former roommate took off for the Ukraine. And of course there were the weddings. Even though she'd moved away, her mother mentioned each invitation that arrived at their house.

Marnie still went to church every Sunday, but not to the singles ward, where the men were just as strange and insistent as the ones at BYU. She went to the regular neighborhood ward and taught nursery. Every week she would prepare her lessons: "I am Grateful for my Eyes," or "Music Makes Me Happy." On Sundays she played ring-around-the-rosy, blew bubbles, sang "Once There Was a Snowman." When the snowman melted, small, small, small, she would make herself as tiny as she could, wrap her arms around her knees, and tuck herself up hard as a nut. The children would climb all over her, pulling on her shoulders and grabbing at her hair, until she would pop her head up and grin and spring back to life. The children screamed with laughter. At church, Marnie had no real friends her own age.

She came home from work every night, poured herself a Sprite, and sat at the window watching the empty sidewalk, waiting for her future to present itself. She liked to think she'd been led, for some reason, to find a copy of the Southern Utah *Spectrum* curiously left behind at the Great Clips where her hair had been cut. After seeing the ad for River City Mortgage and Financial, she'd gotten the job easily, after a simple phone interview. And her apartment was cheap and clean and reasonable, available for occupancy in the middle of the month. The stars' aligning in such a way had to indicate divine providence. Didn't it? This seemed the only reasonable explanation since, her protests to her mother notwithstanding, she *didn't* know what she was doing in Cedar City. It seemed only right that God would.

But she didn't meet a man; she didn't have an accident; she didn't befriend a wise, elderly neighbor. She woke up every morning at 6:45, got dressed, and drove herself to the mortgage company. She went to the movies with friendly acquaintances. She took black-and-white photos of bare-limbed trees and old houses. She gained ten pounds. Finally, after months of suspense, something happened. God's hand, she believed, had finally tilted toward her, and she trembled with relief.

Marnie came home from church one sunny Sunday afternoon and found her sister Tina perched on her doorstep, sitting on top of a rolled-up sleeping bag.

"Look what the cat dragged in," Tina said.

They went inside and dumped Tina's things on the futon in the living room. Marnie poured both of them a Sprite. They sat together at the glass-topped kitchen table and Tina emptied her pockets on its surface, letting the pennies and nickels and dimes roll around and spill onto the floor.

"This," Tina said, "is it. Nowhere to go but up."

"That's a good way to look at it," Marnie said.

Tina didn't look bad at all. She'd always been the most beautiful sister: her vivid green eyes, her skin as smooth and taut as a Barbie doll's. Beside her Marnie always felt swollen and overdressed. Tina yawned and stretched her long brown arms above her head in a way that seemed so easy and relaxed to Marnie, considering her situation. Almost literally penniless, wandering, coming to Marnie, of all people—the sister who shouldn't be able to stand her own self. She didn't want to appear too anxious that Tina would stay. She wanted to seem an unthreatening solution.

"I hate to ask you this," Tina said, "but I need a place to crash. For a few days, or weeks maybe. I don't know."

Marnie tried to seem measured. Contemplative. "Why not?" she said. "I mean, yeah. Sure."

Her heart thrummed inside her with the thrill of purposeful-

97

ness. She decided not to ask any questions, not about Jimmy or California or how Tina even got there in the first place. She reached her hand across the table and laid it lightly atop her sister's.

"Whatever you need."

"Thank you," Tina said. "Truly."

They each had their conditions. Tina's was, don't tell Mom and Dad I'm here till I say so. Marnie's was, don't lie to me. It worked for a while. Tina had been there for a few days sleeping on the futon when a guy from church told Marnie about a cashier position at his hardware store. Tina took the job, working the noon-to-seven shift. Since Marnie usually got off work first, she started making sure dinner was on the table when Tina came home. She would plan menus and write them in her day planner: spaghetti, chicken tacos, tuna-noodle casserole. One Sunday she actually cooked a roast, with potatoes and carrots and gravy made from scratch. Tina always did the dishes. Then they sat together on the futon watching cable television until ten-thirty or eleven.

"You sound so much happier," her mother said when she called. "Have you met a boy?"

"Let's just say that I have more company than I used to," she answered. Marnie loved being coy with her mother, stringing her along. She wasn't sure if she felt guilty about this.

Sometimes when her mother called, Tina would poke Marnie in the side or stick out her tongue or do silent impressions of their mother's "chatty face," as they liked to call it, trying to get Marnie to laugh. Whenever their mother started talking about Tina, Marnie rolled her eyes in her sister's direction, a signal saying, "Here we go again." Her mother thought Tina was still in California, living with "that guitarist in some crazy band." She usually heard from Tina only every month or so, and she hadn't started getting too suspicious. Marnie even lied once outright, telling her mother, "I've talked to her, she's fine, she says hello."

Then, after living with Marnie for almost a month, Tina began missing dinner.

"Me and some friends went out after work," Tina explained, coming home to a chugging dishwasher, a fridge full of Tupperware containers.

Ungrateful! Marnie thought. *Inconsiderate!*

One night she watched as Tina hitched a denim skirt around her hips and spritzed herself with Marnie's body spray.

"So who are these people you're going out with?" Marnie asked.

"You're just as bad as Mom," Tina sighed. She laced up her pair of thick brown boots and strode to the door without even looking at Marnie's expression. Without even waiting for her to respond.

Marnie walked out onto the apartment's tiny balcony. The night was turning blue and dark, and she could just make out her sister's form trudging across the parking lot, heading for a rumbling pickup waiting in the street.

"Don't you ever say that!" she screamed into her sister's rigid back. "Ever!"

For days afterward neither sister spoke to the other. Marnie stopped doing Tina's laundry. She deliberately changed the channel when she could tell Tina was watching something. She made meals for one.

Then one night Tina didn't come home at all. Marnie sat on the futon waiting, trying to watch late-night television, but all the shows were either infomercials or recreations of gory crime-scene investigations replete with foreboding background music. "Little did she know," the ominous voice-over guy intoned, "that this would be her fatal mistake."

She turned off the television and let the darkness surround her. Her sister was out there in the world, beyond her, doing secret things. When she began crying she decided not to stop it. She pushed the sobs out from her chest and let herself wail until she choked, until she was afraid she might stop breathing. She balled her fists and ground them into her thighs. She shuddered and moaned. She cried so long she slipped right into sleep without noticing. She woke up at 6:45, achy and stiff, to the sound of her alarm clock buzzing in the bedroom. That morning, she called in sick.

By ten o'clock, Marnie was driving north on I-15 in the left-hand lane, five miles over the speed limit, her windows rolled down. She wanted to feel the world coming at her: the rush of wind blasting through her hair, the sounds of cars hurtling past, the thick, acrid mixture of tires and asphalt and speed and heat.

It hadn't taken her long that morning to discover her responsibility. She needed to head home and tell. She imagined sitting on the couch with her mother, holding both of her hands. She would keep nothing back, telling everything she'd lied about and everything she'd tried, explaining the way things seemed to be just turning hopeful for Tina before crumbling. She would say that she understood all her mother's frustrations and that the two of them were in this thing together now. *We've got to have faith that someday she'll come around*, she imagined herself saying; and her mother crying, maybe, or just holding her tight and strong, the two of them united in resolve and frustrated love for Tina.

Pulling into her parents' driveway, she saw the front door open wide, the way her mother liked it in the summer. Only the glass storm door stood between the living room and the world outside. Her mother opened doors, opened windows, raised blinds as high as they could go until they bowed in the middle.

Marnie jogged up the concrete steps and onto the front porch. The afternoon sun slanted against the front of the house. She cupped her hands around her eyes, shielding them from the glare, and pressed her face against the cool glass door just like she had as a child.

She saw them before they even knew she was there: the backs of both their heads as they sat together on the couch, Tina leaning against her mother's shoulder, her mother's hand stroking Tina's hair. Marnie stood, watching, frozen. Then they sensed her, both of them together, and turned to see her standing there gaping. When she saw Tina's swollen cheek and the gash underneath her right eye, Marnie understood, instantly, the meaning of the hard set of her mother's mouth. It was an expression reserved specifically for her, perhaps one reserved by mothers for oldest sisters the world over, a particular mixture of disappointment and blame. *Why weren't you watching her?* it demanded. *Irresponsible!* it said.

Marnie turned her burning face away from them, afraid they would see her shock and guilt and anger, and started down the stairs. She heard Tina calling to her through the glass—"Marnie!"—and she paused on the bottom step. But before she could turn around she heard her mother's voice.

"Let her go."

But she couldn't go. She tried to. She jumped into her car and screeched away from the house. She took the southbound freeway on-ramp, but that was as far as she could get and she circled the cloverleaf back around north. The more she thought, the angrier she got. Always, always, she was the one to walk away from a fight; always she had been the swallower of words. What good had it done her? What joy or grace or good will had she won? She deserved her turn at exploding. It was her time to make a mess and see everyone around her scuttling, rushing, cleaning it all up.

She careened into the driveway too fast and one tire went into a flower bed, but she didn't care; she yanked the parking brake and left it. She stormed up the stairs and flung open the front door, but no one was there to witness her resolve and her fury. A few moments passed as she stood, waiting and looking, feeling the red heat draining from her face and the pace of her heart slowing.

"Hey!" she said. Her voice rang through the silent house.

Then her mother appeared from the kitchen. She had a glass of lemonade and a plate of Ritz crackers and sliced cheddar cheese.

"That's for her, I see," Marnie said.

"It is. She's hurt. She's hungry. I told her to go upstairs and rest and I'd bring her something."

"So that's it? After everything, you're just tucking her in, bringing her crackers? Do you have any idea what she's been doing?"

Marnie's mother raised her eyebrows. "A better idea than you do, I'd wager."

"So that's what this is all about. This is all *my* fault. Never mind she's the one running around in the middle of the night, hanging out with boys who beat her up and crazy people on drugs, ruining everyone's lives. I lie a little—for a good reason, a real purpose—and suddenly I'm the bad one? It's my fault now she got hurt, like I should have been watching her better? Like worse things than this didn't happen when you were supposedly in charge?"

"I don't have time for this," her mother said, and started up the stairs. But halfway up, she turned around and faced her daughter.

"Please," she said slowly. "Just understand. This has nothing to do with you."

Marnie's childhood room sat waiting for her. She climbed into the bed she'd slept in almost all her life and rolled herself up into a ball. Her body throbbed with spent emotion and she didn't have the energy to take off her shoes. She hadn't taken much with her to Cedar City. Evidence of the life she had lived thus far remained here, in this room. Tacked all over the wall was proof of her good intentions: ribbons from the Reflections contest; prom pictures with Marnie in stiff and uncomfortable dresses, holding hands with stiff and uncomfortable boys; posters with inspirational sayings ("When you can't stand it . . . then kneel"); her Young Womanhood theme ("We are daughters of our Heavenly Father who loves us and we love him."); and Christ, wise and masculine in his scarlet robe, his patient gray eyes looking down on her, knowing her heart.

Everybody suffers, he seemed to be saying. *All of us.*

Tina must have slipped in beside her in the night, softly, quiet enough not to wake her. As the morning came and Marnie started rising out of sleep, it didn't feel strange to have her sister's warm body curled up against her; it felt familiar, like when they were children and would sneak into each other's beds in the night, giggling, excited about having their own little plans and hatching them. She felt Tina's warm breath along her neck. She listened to her exhalations, each like a tiny sigh.

The sun shafted through the blinds, and in each finger of light Marnie could see dust tumbling, visible, invisible, then visible again. In the dimness of the morning, Tina's unlined face looked as if it had been sculpted from a cool, smooth stone, like granite or ivory save for the skin around her eye, which was swollen and red. Soon, Marnie knew, the bruising would appear, and the colors would emerge: first a purple deep as night, then fading into blue and dusty gray, and ringed along the bottom with yellow and earthy green. So many lovely colors, Marnie thought, all living there just under our skin, waiting to be revealed.

She wanted to touch her sister, to smooth her fingers along the pain that had bloomed across Tina's face. But she didn't want to wake her. She didn't want to talk. Instead she let her hand hover just above her sister's skin. She caught her light, warm breathing in her palm. She turned and faced the morning.

Beth—1996

cs

WHO DO YOU THINK YOU ARE?

The tardy bell rang five minutes ago and Mr. Glassing still hasn't shown up. Every day for the last six months I've known exactly where to find him: standing in front of the chalkboard marking off our names on the roll, handing out his "how ya doin's" and "good to see ya's." He likes to watch us all come in so we don't get out of control before class starts, and it works. There's never much messing around here in seventh period Honors English 9. And now he's gone five minutes and everybody's acting crazy, sitting on top of their desks and shouting across the room. It's a zoo. Mr. Glassing would be so disappointed.

"He's bailed for sure," my good friend Rhonda says, and she looks all happy about it. Pleased as punch, as my mom would say. I want to strangle her. "I bet we could just leave and we wouldn't even get in trouble."

I don't respond. I keep my eyes on the door, my ears tuned in to catch the sound of his footsteps in the hall.

"Hello in there?" Rhonda says. I turn and look at her, trying to keep my face expressionless. She sighs and stalks away from me, over to a group of girls sitting on an empty book cart. But I don't care. It's better, anyway, that she doesn't know. If she did she would either faint or die laughing, and today's been such a hard day already that I don't think I could handle either. So let her think I'm a goody-goody. A kid obsessed with following the rules. Because how could I tell her? A *teacher*? Mr. Glassing? Rhonda even makes fun of him, hooking her thumb through her belt loop like he sometimes does and strolling around, waving her free hand in the air and saying, "Iambic pen*tameter*. The rhythm of the *Gods*," which most kids think is hilarious. I never laugh but it doesn't seem to stop her. She can be oblivious when she wants to be.

But it's good she doesn't know my secret. Nobody does, not even him. Sometimes I feel like a blinking neon sign whenever he comes within five feet of me, but so far, most people seem to think I like him in the way a kid's supposed to like a teacher. I respect him, I look up to him, I want to make him proud of me. Nobody's asked me, "Hey, Beth. Do you love him?" And if they did, I don't think I could deny it. I would have to say, Yes, I admit it. You've got me. I'm in love with my teacher, nine years older than me. It would be shocking, I know, and inappropriate and wrong. But I also think it might feel good to say it out loud: I love Brian Glassing. I love Brian Glassing. Terrible and wonderful and true.

I met Mr. Glassing six months ago, the first day of my ninth grade year. I walked into class and saw him standing in front of the chalkboard, his legs straddled wide like a guitarist in a band, his hands stuffed all casual in his pockets. He had a shaggy goatee, not clipped and groomed like most guy teachers', and he wore a T-shirt with a picture of Shakespeare on it underneath his blazer.

"People!" he said, and Rhonda rolled her eyes. She absolutely hates it when teachers call us "people." She says it's rude.

"First thing, no screwing around. Understand? This is serious business in here. Words are serious. Poetry is serious. These guys and these ladies," he said, sweeping his arm in an arc along the *Authors of the World* display hanging around the room, "they are serious. You will not disrespect them, or me, or each other. You good?"

A couple of spiky-haired boys sitting next to me laughed into their hands. Mr. Glassing didn't seem to notice.

"So. Seating chart."

Everybody groaned.

"Where's the trust?" Rhonda asked, but Mr. Glassing acted like he didn't hear her.

"Today," he said, "The alphabet starts with the letter *P*. For Positivity. For Perseverance. And for a Passion for Poetry and Prose. All qualities that I hope you will diligently strive to obtain."

He paused, smiling. He seemed to be half joking. Making fun of himself. Some of the kids in class weren't buying it but everyone was listening.

"Just because you've always done a thing one way doesn't mean that you can't mix it up. Change it. Bend the rules. Like the Alphabet. Who says we always have to start with *A*?"

We all looked at each other, a little confused. Were we supposed to answer this question?

"I mean, who says?" He moved his gaze around the perimeter of the room where we all stood with our books clutched against our chests, none of us saying a word. "Okay, then," he said. "Palmer, Elizabeth." He slapped his hand on the desk right across from his.

The name, of course, was mine. I slid into my seat and he looked at me straight on for a couple seconds. His eyes were green and alive.

"El numero uno," he said. The number one. For the first time in my memory, my name was called first at school.

So all my problems started this morning, when Mr. Glassing decided to show a movie called *Ordinary People* in his honors classes without sending home parental permission slips. Here in Utah, rated-R movies are huge no-no's. Even a lot of parents don't watch them, and those who do usually feel a little guilty about it, since everybody knows it's more or less against Church rules. It's not a *commandment* really, like "Thou shalt not steal," or "Thou shalt not commit adultery." It's more like a really powerful suggestion, such as not mowing your lawn in your bikini, which a neighbor of mine, Mrs. Probert, did for about three weeks one summer until she started getting notes of complaint left in her mailbox.

Mr. Glassing first tried showing the movie in second period. Unfortunately for him, Katie Carmichael and Julia DeOlivero—tattletales, both of them—are in that class. Jordan Fronk's in second period too—a kid who recently tried to start a petition to ban Coke from school premises because it contains caffeine and is therefore against the Word of Wisdom. Apparently the three of them met in a huddle after class, marched to the principal's office in a self-righteous huff, and blew the story open.

By lunchtime the whole honors crowd knew what had gone down. All the kids at my table were buzzing, but I could barely swallow my peanut butter sandwich. We found out that the principal, Mr. Dunning, had called Mr. Glassing to his office right in the middle of third period and let him have it. Katie and Julia retold the story to anybody who would listen.

"Molly Mormon butt-kissers," Rhonda said. Rhonda is Catholic and has very little patience with the rest of us. "Did you know that Jordan Fronk says his mom is coming later today? I guess she's getting together with some other moms and they're bringing a list."

"What?" I said. "A list of all the ways that Mr. Glassing has taught us and sacrificed for us and basically made English fun instead of boring and painful?"

"You wish," Rhonda said. "I'm sure it's your basic Mormon Lady list: this book had swearing, that story had a pregnant teenager, and stop setting a bad example by not wearing socks with your shoes."

I suggested that we start our own petition in support of Mr. Glassing, but none of the other kids at the table seemed too excited about it. Most of them, in fact, were just ticked at being cheated out of the chance to watch a video in class which, rated-R or not, is a luxury never to be messed with.

But I was nervous. What if Mr. Glassing got in real trouble? What if he got so mad that he decided to heck with all of us? It was embarrassing, sometimes, being these sheltered Mormon kids who never got to experience Real Life or understand True Art. I could tell Mr. Glassing felt sorry for us. He grew up in Chicago and had backpacked in Europe and visited Japan and settled here, he said, because he liked to mountain bike and ski.

"I had no idea," he would often say in class, and then go on to tell a story about liquor laws or stores closed on Sunday or Republican city councils. Most kids in class liked these stories and encouraged them, not because they particularly enjoyed our state being mocked, but because anytime you can get a teacher on a topic that doesn't relate to actual learning it's a bonus.

But the stories worried me. I wanted him to like Utah, to like Mormons. To like me. To never leave.

I knew that during fourth period Mr. Glassing had the Regulars —not the honors kids, not even the college-prep kids, but the lowest on the totem pole before you hit remedial—and that he had second lunch, so he'd still be in the classroom. The conversation at the lunch table had turned. Mr. Glassing's little scandal had been forgotten already and dismissed like yesterday's news, but I couldn't get him out of my head. I had to go to him and make sure he was okay. I stood up from the table.

"Hey, Beth! Where you going?" Rhonda yelled.

"Nowhere!" I said, tossing my lunch in the trash. "I mean, I forgot something. I need to do something."

Class time was almost over, and I had only a few minutes to get to his room on the other side of the building. I knew if I could see him, watch him teaching for just a minute, I would know if he was okay. I can tell his moods really easily now—just one look, one certain gesture, like how he clenches and unclenches his hands when we're getting on his nerves. Before I got to his room I could hear his voice filling up the hall.

"Your time is up," he was saying. I was so relieved to hear it I

109

didn't care how tense he sounded.

I peeked around his door and saw him whipping up and down the aisles, snatching worksheets from students' desks. Grammar worksheets, I could see. The kids in the room were all quiet and looked just a little bit afraid—quite a feat, considering they're the Regulars —and I knew right away that Mr. Glassing was mad. Grammar worksheets were a dead giveaway. He hates them and tells us so and, so far, has only threatened to use them as a punishment. I watched as he stalked around the classroom, tight-lipped, silent, daring the kids to make a sound. He was punishing them—and through them, all of us—for our narrow-mindedness, our clenched-up sensibilities.

When the bell rang he didn't even say good-bye to his class. He just sat at his desk scowling down at the papers in front of him, passionately circling all the errors with a felt-tipped red pen. I stood there, shifting in my shoes, while his students pushed past me. But then I thought, "Do it, Beth. If you're going to do it, do it."

"Mr. Glassing?" I said.

He looked up, seemingly surprised to see me in the doorway.

"I just wanted to tell you we're not all like that. Like Katie and Julia and Jordan. Some of us appreciate art. Some of us don't tell on people."

He tilted his head at me in a tender kind of way. He breathed in through his nose and let a slow sigh out his chest. Then he smiled.

"You're one of the good ones, Beth. It's kids like you. This is why I do it, you know? For kids like you."

His eyes were soft and heavy and sad, and I wanted to go to him, to hold out my arms and watch him fold into them. I wanted to say, "I understand, I understand," smooth his hair, feel his heart beating. Instead I stood for a few hot seconds in the silence, looking into his face until I couldn't stand it anymore and had to look down.

"I'll see you seventh period," I said.

"See you then."

And he bent back over his desk, his red pen suspended, busy with correction.

This is why I love Mr. Glassing:

He's kind. He gives students his home phone number to call if they have questions or problems or just want to talk. I've called twice with supposed homework questions and he was very pleasant and patient on the phone both times. He has two cats named Elinore and Baby, and he lets both of them sleep in his bed. He helped build a house for Habitat for Humanity last summer.

He's smart. He double-majored in English and philosophy in college and once won an essay contest about Thoreau. (Or Emerson. I keep getting them confused. The one who went off into the woods.) He uses words like "parsimonious" and "fruition" and makes it seem natural.

He's handsome, but not in an obvious kind of way. His nose is a little on the big side, but I'm okay with it because it makes him look regal and unique. He has long, sensitive fingers, like you'd find on a painter or a pianist. His eyes literally change color: green some days, then gray, sometimes a mossy hazel. He smiles with his whole face.

He listens to the same kind of music I listen to, older bands like Depeche Mode and The Cure. During our poetry unit he let us bring songs we liked, lyrically, and he played them during journal free-writing time. He picked some of his favorite songs and typed the words up for a handout so we could understand that poetry isn't just written by boring dead white guys.

He told me that I'm bright. In front of the whole class. He'd asked a question about *The Lord of the Flies*, something about symbolism and the pig's head on a stick and the nature of evil, and when none of us raised our hands he looked right at me and said, "Beth, you're so bright, you should have no trouble figuring this one out." When I answered it I must have impressed him because he said, "See? There you go."

Sometimes, when he comes up behind me to check my work, he puts his hands on my shoulders. He hardly ever does this to anyone else.

So all that history brings me to this moment: sitting here in seventh period, waiting for him to show, fear and anticipation wrestling around in my stomach. When I finally hear footsteps coming down the hall, they're flat and heavy and slow. It's easy to tell they're not Mr. Glassing's. I recognize the guy who comes into the room but I don't know his name. He's big and redheaded, sweaty on his forehead, a shop guy or a coach.

"Settle!" he shouts.

A kid on the front row asks, "Where's Mr. Glassing?"

Mr. Shop Guy glares at him. "The million-dollar question. All I know is it's my prep period, and the last thing I want to do is hang out up here babysitting all of you because your teacher had a temper tantrum."

There's a bit of spit collected in the corners of his mouth. His teeth are gray.

"This is English class, right? So read a book. Write a poem. Diagram a sentence. Whatever it is you do in here, do it quiet. All right?"

It doesn't take much, usually, to scare an honors crowd into silence. Everybody reaches into his backpack to pull out paper and pencils and books. Except me. I refuse to move. The substitute sinks down into Mr. Glassing's chair with a grunt. He's four feet away from me and I think I can smell his breath.

"Hey," he says to me. "If you're just going to sit there gazing off, at least put a book in front of your face and pretend to do something."

I look him right in the eye. I'm not afraid of this tough guy, this imposter. I don't want him to be here any more than he does.

"So you got something to do?" he asks.

I don't even hesitate. I don't even think.

"As a matter of fact, I do." Then I stand up, turn my back on him and make my way to the door.

"Beth," I hear Rhonda hissing. "What are you doing?"

I don't turn around and answer. I just go.

I'm a pretty good kid. I'm the youngest in a family of three girls and my nickname at home is "Lo-Main," short for low maintenance. My mom and dad and me, we actually like each other, which is pretty rare, I know. My dad has always been a softy, and my mom's undergone some kind of metamorphosis—maybe it has to do with menopause—and has given up on being strict now that I'm the only one left at home. Not that they let me do whatever I want or anything. I have curfews, some chores. But I think my mom is over being ultra-vigilant by now. She basically breathed right down my other sisters' necks most of their adolescence and got, as she likes to say, mixed results. So I don't think she has any energy left to be suspicious. And I don't give her many reasons to worry. I play clarinet in the school band; I get good grades; she knows most of my friends and my friends' families. I've never had a boyfriend. She comes to my room sometimes at night and flops on my bed and wants to talk about friends and feelings and if there's anything I need to get off my chest, and then I usually tell her a thing or two so she feels like she's doing her job. Then she leaves me alone until the mood strikes her again. It's our system. It works pretty well for both of us.

But I wonder what she'll say to me tonight. I'm sure they're going to call her. I've never been suspended—I've never even had a teacher call with anything but good news—but I can imagine how the conversation might go.

"Mrs. Palmer?" they'll say. "Your daughter Beth walked right out of Honors English 9, and nobody has seen her since. We think she left the building."

And then my mom will faint.

Although I haven't left the building, not yet. Right now I'm sitting on the toilet in the girls' bathroom so I can contemplate my next move. I can't go back to class—that much is certain. What I need is information. What happened to Mr. Glassing? Where has he gone?

And then, like a miracle, my answer appears. Jordan's mom, Mrs. Fronk, comes swinging into the bathroom with her little gang of ladies. I can see them through the crack in the bathroom door, and they all look flushed and beaming and thrilled. I tuck my feet up so they can't see me.

"I say, 'Good Riddance,'" says a freckly blonde.

"It's about time," another woman answers. She opens the door to the stall next to mine.

"Who will protect the children if not the parents? The government? Never. Hide their heads in the sand—that's what they do. The unions pay them to do it," says Freckly.

"It's enough to make a person want to homeschool," Mrs. Fronk says.

I sit on my toilet seat and listen to them. With each passing moment I get more and more concerned. Good riddance? What, exactly, does this mean?

"That teacher never said a word," Mrs. Fronk says. "Not one word in his own defense. Now, that's the behavior of a person with a guilty conscience, if you ask me."

"I don't know," says the voice in the stall next to mine. "He didn't look too guilty to me."

"More like mad," says Freckly.

"Did you see the way he looked at Mr. Dunning? If looks could kill, I tell you what."

"Well, whether or not he knows that he's guilty isn't the point," says Mrs. Fronk, rubbing her hands under the drying machine. "The point is, he's gone. And we didn't even have to get him fired. He left of his own free will and accord, and that's just great by me."

I think I'm going to be sick. If they could only see themselves like I see them: ridiculous in their Wal-Mart clothes, their ten-dollar haircuts. They think they have some kind of right to march into my life and kink it all out of joint? They think they're righteous or something? I see their faces. I can see the thrill in their eyes, the joy they took in making him squirm. Just who do they think they are?

Then I remember what Mr. Glassing always told us: Be passionate. Be daring. Go with your gut. So I will. I will. I know what I've got to do.

114

I know where Mr. Glassing lives. It's a little blue house with dingy shutters and a falling-down carport in North Salt Lake. I've been here three times. It's creepy, I know, like I'm a stalker or something. And I've even done stalkerish things, like sitting on a bench at the park across the street pretending to read a magazine while I wait for his car to pull in the driveway, or opening his mailbox to see what's inside it. Once, when nobody was home, I even dared to go right to the front door and peek through the living room window, and I saw his couch and the outline of his dining room table. All three times I came here I just told my mom I was going to Rhonda's, but then I walked out the door, caught a bus, and rode my way to his house. The first time was the scariest—two connections and I got a little lost in his neighborhood, which isn't the best part of town—but each time I did it, I felt better. I crept along these unfamiliar sidewalks with my hair hanging down over my face, shielding my eyes, and it was like I was invisible but powerful, a featureless, nameless girl who was liable to do anything. Anything!

He's never seen me here. But today is the day. How alone he must feel, abandoned, betrayed. And angry, of course, angry, and I need to talk him out of any rash decisions. I can convince him; I'm sure of it. If only he'll listen to me, he will understand how important he is to me and to all of us, how without him, nothing will ever be the same.

I sit on the park bench across the street from his house and I can see his Chevy parked in the carport. Some little Hispanic kids are playing inside the plastic tunnels and slides at the park behind me, shrieking and yelling, ignoring their mother who wants them to come down. She's threatening them in Spanish, counting to three. "Uno! Dos! Tres!" she keeps yelling. They aren't listening to her. I decide she's counting for me. Spurring me on. The next countdown's mine.

"Uno!" she cries. Her face is red, insistent.

"Dos!" The children are laughing at her, hiding somewhere up in the tunnel beyond her reach.

"Tres!" I stand up.

115

A car splashes along the rain-wet road and I wait for it. I keep my eyes on Mr. Glassing's door as it passes. Then I walk, my heartbeat steady and loud, my feet keeping even time like a marching soldier. I don't give myself a minute to stop or think or question. I raise up my hand and I knock.

Silence. Quiet. I peer inside the window. The house is dark and motionless. Behind me, the Hispanic women and her children trudge down the sidewalk, away from the park and from me. I'm alone on the street. Even the wind has stopped blowing, and the world is still: the trees, the air, the clouds in the sky. I feel like I'm a girl in a movie and people are watching me, hushed and expectant.

I ring the doorbell and hear the chime echoing inside his walls. Just when I think no one is coming, I hear the thump of footsteps. My heart picks up speed.

The door opens. A strange, skinny guy in a tank top peers around the door at me, suspicious. His hair is curly and wild, and I wonder if I just woke him up.

"Yeah?" he says.

I start to say excuse me, wrong house, somehow, wrong guy, but then I remember. Donnie! It's Donnie! The new guy, the roommate who just came to live with him, an old friend from college who's trying to break into the world of professional snowboarding. He works as a bartender. Sleeps all day. Of course!

"Donnie?" I say. My voice sounds very small. I keep my hands tucked behind my back so he won't see them shaking. "Is that right?"

"Yeah," he says again, but slower this time.

"Is Mr. Glassing here?" I say. "I mean, Brian? Is he home?"

Donnie leans out the door and looks up and down the street. "How did you get here?"

"A bus. Well, a couple of buses," I say. He continues to look at me expectantly. "I took a transfer?" I explain, and laugh nervously.

"And how old are you?"

I realize there's no point in lying. He's onto me already.

"Fourteen."

"Hmm," he grunts. "You from school?"

I nod.

"So you know that Brian's pissed?"

So Mr. Glassing *is* home. He's already told Donnie the whole story. "Yes," I say. "I just wanted to talk to him. Tell him we're all really sorry. Tell him he needs to come back to school tomorrow."

"Well good luck with that!" Donnie laughs. He leans against the doorframe, filling up the space.

"So can I talk to him?"

"Oh. Sorry. He's not here. Took off for a minute. He'll be back, though. Pretty soon. You want to wait?" He gestures inside the house.

I pause. I think, *Strange man, empty house, no witnesses, missing girl.*

"I'm just heading out. Leaving right now," he says. He jangles a set of keys in his hand. "But you're welcome to wait."

I wonder where this Donnie is heading, looking like he just rolled out of bed. "You're sure?"

"No problem. Just chill. He'll be back any minute." Then he swings his arm out and lets me inside Mr. Glassing's house. Without even giving me a backward glance, he skips down the front stairs, twirling his keys on his finger. Before I know it he's gone.

And now I'm alone in Mr. Glassing's house. I sit very quietly on his saggy plaid couch. I've always known Mr. Glassing isn't a materialistic person, but looking around this place I'm even more sure of it. There's nothing in his living room but this ancient sofa, a couple of beanbag chairs, and a boxy old television with rabbit ears. No plants. No stereo system. I crane my neck so I can see into his kitchen, and at least he's hung a poster in there: a print of that famous screaming guy, with the melty face and bugged-out eyes. I wish I could remember who painted it, or what it's called. Talking about the poster could be an icebreaker. A point of discussion.

I sit patiently for what seems like a long time, running possible conversation starters through my mind. *Guess who? Just thought I'd stop by! I bet you never thought you'd see me here!* At least a half hour goes by before I realize I've got to go to the bathroom, but I'm a little afraid to stand up. I know it's irrational, but I feel like I might trip some alarm, or Mr. Glassing might walk in at that exact moment and think I'm in here to ransack his place. But when you've got to go, you've got to go. I stand. Nothing happens.

I creep to the bathroom and push the door open. A film of soap and dust coats the counter. The shower curtain is swept back, and I notice the floor of the tub is gray and unscrubbed. I'm sure if I leaned over I could carve my initials in it with my fingernail. I don't let myself think about the toilet and how long it has gone without a good cleaning.

When I stand at the sink to wash my hands I look at the items Mr. Glassing has lined up along the counter—shaving cream, a plugged up razor, deodorant, a comb—and before I know what's gotten into me, I pick up each one and turn it over in my hands. I squirt a pillow of shaving cream into my palm and rub it between my fingers, and when I bring my hands up to my nose, I smell spicy and sharp, like a man.

I look at my face in the mirror and pretend he's waiting just outside the door for me. I pull his comb through my own dark hair and study my face from different angles. My cheeks are too round and my lips are too narrow, but if I tilt my chin a certain way and push my mouth out, I look better. Suddenly his cats, Baby and Elinore, appear. They slide up against my shins purring. I reach down to pet them.

"Hello, kitties," I whisper. "Hello girls."

They saunter out of the bathroom and down the hall, and I follow them into what must be Mr. Glassing's bedroom. His clothes lie in little mounds all over the floor. I check out the window. No one is coming. I stand very still and listen, and I can't hear a thing. I am alone here, I tell myself. No one will know.

I lie down on his unmade bed. His pillowcase needs washing, but I bury my face in it just the same and the scent of him—new paper, wet ground—rises up and into me.

I close my eyes and then I hear it. A car, slowing and turning. I scramble out of bed and see a blue Volkswagen pulling into the driveway. Mr. Glassing is inside it; and driving, a woman with curly blonde hair.

I've been sitting in Mr. Glassing's closet for close to fifteen minutes, too scared to listen to them very well. My heart is pounding in my ears, my hands are shaking, and I'm thinking, *What will I do or say if they find me?* A fourteen-year-old girl, crazy and pathetic, crammed in among my English teacher's loafers and tennis shoes for no explainable reason. But it seems as if they're not coming in here after all. At least not yet. And I know that I've got to get out of here before they do, because even if they don't open the closet I couldn't bear listening to what might go on.

I open the closet door and start to stand. Then I hear him say, "These kids," and I can tell he's angry. He's talking to this woman—I have heard her name, it's Marianne—about us. About me.

"These kids," he says, "they're like little robots. No thinking for themselves! No self-expression. I can't stand it."

"But if you just stick it out three more months, Brian. Think about it. Do you really want this on your record? Quitting and everything? You know you want to teach college, and if you just up and quit it'll look bad."

"But I'm climbing the walls in there, Marianne. These kids look up at me with their big, dumb, glazed-over expressions, and I think, 'Dupes! All of you!' It's sad, is what it is. I feel like, anymore, teaching them is just a waste of time."

"It's not a waste."

"It is! It is! They think they've got everything figured out, you know. They look at me with those sour little judgmental eyes."

"Every last one of them?"

"Every last one."

"Come on."

"I mean it. If there was one kid—even one—that I thought was worth fighting for, I'd stay. But you know what? To hell with them. To hell with all of them."

119

I can't believe it's Mr. Glassing—*my* Mr. Glassing—in there talking. I want to pound my fist against his bedroom wall. I want to yell *Shut up!* to make him stop, to make him realize that he's ruining everything. Who is this girl? Why are you trying to impress her? Why are you lying to her, telling her things you don't really believe, acting nothing like the man I know you are: kind, good, patient, open-hearted? You looked at me, Mr. Glassing, and you told me things with your eyes. Don't deny it! That you were proud of me, that I was smart, that you were glad to see me every day and teach me and that you saw great things in my future. "Teaching is the greatest job on earth," you told us, and we *believed* you. "Call me," you said. "Anytime. I care about you guys." And you did, you do, I swear it.

"Mormons are impossible," Marianne says. "You know this. There's no changing them."

"Free me from their clutches!" he says, and she giggles, high and breathy, like a cheerleader.

I realize now I've got to leave. I'm afraid I'm going to cry and he will hear me. I sneak out into the hall.

"But you don't want to let them ruin your career," she says. I see them together on the couch, his arm slung around her shoulder like he owns her, her body curled into his. "All they want from you is a little apology, a little yessir, nossir, you're right, I'm wrong. You can suck it up and go back there in the morning. Torture those kids with worksheets and spelling tests. It'll bore them to tears and keep you safe. Then you can come back home to me every night, and I'll make things all good again."

"Promise?" he says.

"Don't I always make things better?"

She turns toward him and tilts her head up and they kiss. I hear their wet lips parting. The bathroom door stands open, and I see my own reflection in the mirror: small, pale, a sliver of a person. I may as well be a ghost. Who did I think I was, coming here? Trying to claim this man, or save him? He knows nothing about me. I'm here

120

in his house and he can't even tell.

They've stopped talking. I know what they're doing. I stand behind them silent as night. Their heads have disappeared from above the couch, but I can see their legs, intertwined, hanging off the edge. I wonder how long I can stand here staring, breathing, until the sheer force of my presence forces them up and around to look right into my face. I hear his name in my mind: Brian Glassing. Brian Glassing. Loud enough it almost seems outside me. Its rhythm fits the rhythm of my raging heart.

They don't notice me. I walk by them without a sound. I go to his front door and pass through, leaving it open behind me, letting the screen door slam, because if he hears it and comes looking, it won't matter. He won't recognize me. I'll just be a kid on the street with my back to him, walking away from him, some girl he never knew.

Tina—1997

ଔ

TINA'S WEDDING: PART ONE

Tina has arrived in Las Vegas with the man she thinks she loves.
She stands in the wedding chapel at Circus Circus wearing a bright
purple tank top and a denim miniskirt. The top button's undone because she's three months pregnant, and her fiancé, Curtis, has a thick
hand around her waist. Curtis has on a T-shirt that says *Too Many
Freaks, Not Enough Circuses*. They bought it at a garage sale in LaVerkin,
a little town they explored on the trip from Cedar City to Vegas.
They'd been heading straight south along I-15 when Curtis saw the
exit and said, "LaVerkin. What's not to like," so they took the off-
ramp to check it out. They followed the signs and found the garage
sale right away, and the place was hopping: half a dozen ladies rummaging through the clothes bins, some little kids hurtling down the
driveway on wobbly bikes, a spiky-haired teenager pawing through
old records. They met the lady running the sale—Vernetta was her
name—and when they brought her the T-shirt and handed over the
twenty-five cents, she asked where they were headed.

"Vegas," Curtis told her. "The happiest place on earth."

"Isn't Disneyland the happiest place on earth?" Vernetta asked.

"Can a person get married in Disneyland?" Curtis replied. "Don't think so."

Even though Tina was pretty sure a person could. Just not on the spur of the moment, like they are doing. For only $99, they've hooked themselves up with a church and a minister, even a small bouquet of real flowers for Tina to hold. And the wedding chapel at Circus Circus actually isn't as bad as she'd feared. It's like a little mini church, except gaudier than a Mormon chapel, with mini pews padded in green velvet and fake flower arrangements balancing on plastic Roman pillars. The minister is nice too. His name is Edward. He looks to be at least seventy years old, and he's fat and bearded, jolly like Santa Claus.

"Ready to take the leap?" Edward asks them.

"Ready as I'll ever be," Curtis answers. He pulls Tina to him, even closer.

"Young lady?" Edward says.

"Let's hit it," she says, so the minister opens his Bible and reads the verse about a man cleaving unto his wife. Tina faces Curtis and clasps his hands. His eyes are glassy with tears. He loves her so much, she can see it: how he wants to protect her, take care of her. He's a big guy, strong, wide in the neck and shoulders like a cartoon super-hero. But gentle. At least gentle with her.

He wasn't so gentle with Kevin, Tina's ex. Back a year ago, when she and Kevin were still dating, a bunch of friends had gone dancing together. Kevin was drinking too much and accused Tina of flirting around, so Tina started yelling at him in the parking lot and he ex-ploded and hit her. Curtis was just a friend of Tina's at the time—a guy to say hey to a party—but when he caught wind that Kevin was responsible for Tina's wicked black eye, he committed himself to getting revenge. "It's not your deal," Tina told him. "I'm done with him anyway and that's punishment enough." But Curtis wouldn't listen. He tracked Kevin down and pounded him into a bloody mess. Kevin called Tina from the hospital, swearing at her, screaming "cheater" and "whore" into the phone (he was convinced she'd been sleeping with Curtis behind his back and their was no telling him otherwise), and that's how she found out Curtis had gone to Kevin's house in the middle of the night, pulled him out of bed, and beat him so hard his roommate had to call 911. Curtis even got hauled in by the police because of the whole ordeal. But he didn't care, he told Tina. He'd risk a misdemeanor charge any day if it meant taking care of a guy who'd try to hurt her.

Tina started going out with Curtis after that because she thought she owed him one. He wasn't the kind of guy she usually dated: she liked the flashy ones, the big talkers. Her first love, Jimmy, the guy she left in California, was a guitarist in a band. Kevin raced motorcycles. But Curtis was (usually) quiet and low-key. He looked menacing enough with the thick chains clipped to his belt loop, his biceps bursting out of his sleeves. But when he got nervous he spoke so softly that Tina sometimes had to ask him to repeat himself. Like today. Edward the minister has gone through all the vows Tina's heard on TV: have and hold, love and honor, sickness and health, richer and poorer.

"Do you take this woman?" he asks.

"I do," Curtis says quietly. Edward leans in, straining.

"Excuse me?" Edward asks.

Curtis clears his throat. "I do," he says, louder this time. He sniffs and grins at Tina. "I definitely do."

Then it's Tina's turn. She likes the cadence of the whole marriage spiel, the way each vow is coupled with another one, how the minister finishes the whole run-through with a little lilt to his voice as he says "for as long as you both shall live?" She appreciates his saying it that way, instead of "till death do you part," the phrase she'd been taught all her life that Mormon girls hear when they fail. She'd gone to all her church meetings until she was sixteen and her mom stopped trying to force her. She heard all the lessons about temple marriage: how it's an unbreakable covenant, an eternal bond, and when you and your husband kneel at the altar together and see your faces infinitely reflected in the mirrors on either side of the room, you will know you've made the only right choice. She vaguely remembers when the thought of a temple marriage seemed desirable to her, like the ultimate reward for good behavior. But she can't get her head around the idea of "forever" anymore. How would she feel standing next to Curtis in the temple, seeing their reflections repeating back and back and back into eternity, thinking this is it, this is the guy, forever and ever amen? It was hard enough to commit to now. Next year. How did these good Mormon girls commit to eternity?

"Do you take this man?" Edward asks her.

She looks at Curtis's face, his ruddy cheeks and soft chin, his narrowly set eyes. Will her baby look like him? Her baby. Their baby. They'll be a family, the three of them. He begged her to marry him. "Please," he said. "It's only right. I'm not a guy who leaves." She knew he'd stay with her through anything. Over the past year she'd slammed doors on him, kept him waiting, stood him up. Even cheated on him once. And still he hung around, persistent and forlorn as a maltreated puppy. When the pregnancy test came back positive, Tina knew he'd always be a part of her life.

She looks up at the minister, searching his expression for any indication that he knows whether or not this marriage will stick. "Edward," she wants to ask him, "do you think this is a good idea?" She figures he must have developed a kind of hunch about marriage after all these years: whether or not it's worth it, and if it is, if there are certain types who still should never attempt it.

She would ask her own father, if she didn't already know what he would say. Of course he would tell her to marry him.

Get married! he'd say. *A baby deserves a family, a home like the home I gave you, with parents and siblings and piano lessons and homemade casseroles for dinner.*

But Dad, she imagines telling him, *I can't make a home like that! I can't do it!*

And then he would say, *You can try, Tina. When you meet this baby you'll understand that it needs stability and consistency and love. And if there's anything I've taught you, it's that doing right by your family is the only goal worth having in this life.*

And she'd have to agree with him, then. She disagrees with her parents about a lot of things. Church. Politics. What makes a person good or bad, right or wrong. But she knows she was lucky to have a family that loved her, a childhood that made her feel safe and taken care of. Her baby deserves one too.

Tina closes her eyes briefly, a beat longer than a blink. When she opens them she says, "I do," and she hears Edward pronouncing them man and wife, telling Curtis to kiss his bride. He kisses her hard, then sweeps her up in his giant arms and squeezes her so tight that she has to whisper, "Curtis, the baby," in his ear.

"Oops," he says, sheepish, and releases his grip.

"It's okay," Tina says. "Just remember, you know. Be careful."

"Sure," he says. "Yeah."

Suddenly the room fills with music, a tape recording of an organ playing the familiar song that means a wedding's over. This is when they should turn and face the crowd, show their relatives and friends their glowing faces, evidence of their unyielding devotion. But the room is empty, except for Edward and his "legal witness"—a woman named Georgette. She also helped them fill out the paperwork and pressed the button on the tape player. But nobody who cares about them even knows they're in Vegas. Or pregnant. And now, legally and lawfully, married.

"I present Mr. and Mrs. Curtis Gubler," Edward says to the empty room.

"How do you like that, Mrs. Gubler?" Curtis asks. "Tina Marie Gubler?"

She doesn't like it. Gubler. A silly name, like marbles in her mouth.

"Christina Marie," Tina says. "My given name's Christina."

"Really?" He looks shocked.

"After my great-great-grandmother. She was some kind of miracle

127

pioneer baby, I guess. A long story. It's a Palmer family rule that we have one Christina every generation, so I got stuck with it."

"You learn something new every day," Curtis says. "But I like it. Christina. It's pretty. Who knows, maybe this one will be the next generation Christina. Little Christina!" He puts his hand on her stomach and pats it.

"Over my dead body," Tina says.

Georgette bustles over with a camera. "Smile!" she says, and Curtis draws Tina close. The flash goes off, and circles of light swim in front of Tina's eyes.

"We take one of everybody," Georgette says. "You don't have to buy it or anything. Let us know if you want to, though. We can have it ready by tomorrow. Framed and all, if you'd like."

"Great!" Curtis says. "Wonderful!"

But Tina doesn't want it. This is the wedding picture she'll show to her child? Mom in a tank top, Dad in a garage-sale T-shirt, celebrating alone in a fake Vegas church? Maybe a year from now, they'll renew their vows. Have a regular ceremony with a nice dress and a triple-decker cake. She'll even let her mom plan it, if she wants. But maybe her mother won't want to. Maybe she'll say, already married, my dear, already done, just a lot of show for no reason, and then Tina will get angry and they'll have one of their fights and it just won't be worth it.

"I wish I had some rice," Curtis says. "Something to throw."

"It's okay," Tina says. She reminds herself what a good guy he is. How hard he'll try, that he'll be a wonderful father, like her own.

"This I can do," he says, and scoops her up in his arms. She feels tiny and childlike in his embrace, her legs dangling like a doll's. She smells the warm skin on his neck, his sweat and Calvin Klein cologne.

"You got me, Mr. Gubler?" she asks.

"You bet I do," he says, and carries her out of the chapel and into the casino, past the whirring slot machines, the chinking coins, through the mass of gamblers, young and old, rich and poor, hideous and beautiful, all of them hoping the same thing: when the slot machine finally lurches to a stop, when the dealer finally slaps that last card down, that their life will somehow, magically, change.

He pushes her through the crowd to the elevator and presses the button that will take them up to their room. Their marriage bed. Their new life.

"Wait," Tina says. "Before we go up, how about we play a little? A couple hands."

"You think so?" Curtis asks. The elevator yawns open.

"There's a blackjack table over there with my name on it," Tina tells him. "Put me down and let's play. I've got a feeling."

She leaps out of his arms and heads for the table. She doesn't look back. She knows he will follow.

Tildy—1856

൬

CHRISTINA

Late in winter the snow drifts high against the house, and the only sound is the moan of the rocker along the pine floor. Tildy rocks swiftly, up and back, up and back. She is a sharp-faced woman, thin. Her hair is not pinned up. Her face belongs to a woman done with crying. Her eyes are hollow and dry.

In her arms sleeps a limp baby unswaddled from her blanket. The baby is struggling, breathing shallow and high, and her skin is glossy with sweat. From the moment Christina was born she'd been a beautiful baby, everyone said so, the first white baby born in Cache County. The Indians from all around came to Tildy's door to inspect the child's pallor. They whispered that this was not a healthy baby— Tildy couldn't understand their words, but she saw their pinched expressions, the pity in their eyes—and for months she wanted to tell them, *No, no, this one is a healthy one, you just don't know, you have never seen a white baby, they all look this way. Fragile. The color of milk.*

But they were right. She wonders if there's something vital missing from her blood. How else to explain these deaths? But she's watched herself bleed—each time she gives birth there seems to be more of it—and her blood is scarlet and shocking and the same as all the blood she has ever seen: bright with life. So if not in the blood, then where is this weakness hiding? What is it she passes along to her children that dooms them so early, and without exception?

People will ask her, *How did your baby die?*

Froze to death, she wishes she could tell them. *Rolled off the wagon, taken by diphtheria, choked on a button, bit by a rabid dog.* She wants causes. Reasons. Answers.

The people who went on the wagon train from Salt Lake City to Cache County with Tildy and her husband were always asking each other questions about their children. *How many children do you have? How old are your children? What is a mother to do with so many children?* At first they took Tildy for barren. *Who knows the timing of the Lord?* they told her, and repeated the names of all the Bible women crazed with waiting: Sarah, Rachel, Elisabeth the mother of John. Being childless but pregnant, her secret, she let them believe. But then her stomach grew larger. People started treating her like a miracle woman, and she couldn't keep the truth from them anymore. It seemed too much like lying. She stated the truth, laid her hand on her stomach and said, "This is not my miracle," said, "In fact I've birthed four babies previous." Soon the mothers of lost children came to her with their own stories (born blue, smallpox, thrown by a horse) and waited breathlessly for hers.

"They get sick," she tells them. "Don't know how. They grow to be a certain age—laughing, rolling over, grabbing at their own toes —and then they sicken and then they die. Four times. Boy, girl, girl, boy. All of them blonde, except the last one, who had red hair like my father and was strong like him too. So strong I believed the Lord meant for him to remain."

Tildy's husband is a practical man and doesn't like to talk of trouble. "Past is past," he tells her. "I can't divine the future," he also likes to say. He means this as a comfort but it is not. She can't be as he is, living each day as if it were a stone set along a path: one stone, then the next, then the next, each never touching the one before it but all of them together leading to some knowable destination. She envies him.

Her husband has gone back to Salt Lake City to stay with his dying mother, and when he left, Christina was a healthy child. He would wrap his big hands around her middle, stand her on his lap and let her bounce. "She's a strong one," he would say, "strong as they come," and Tildy believed him. Christina had lived longer, already, than any of the others. Already taking to her hands and knees and rocking back and forth, ready to crawl. Her hair had grown into glossy ringlets that covered the tops of her ears. She still nursed two times a night and Tildy let her, loving her fat baby thighs, as warm and soft as new bread.

But now the baby is hot and burning with fever and won't take the breast, won't even open her eyes, and her golden hair is matted with sweat. Her legs hang wilted against Tildy's arm, and it's hard to believe that just a day before these legs had been sturdy and kicking, round from Tildy's milk.

Dawn is coming but the moon is stubborn, hanging frozen in the sky. The snow has stopped falling, and the silence is so deep that Tildy feels buried inside it. She sees nothing outside her window but rolling undulations of snow, dipping and rising like waves, and she feels much as she did on her long voyage from England, looking out into the sea: overwhelmed by distance and emptiness and time. Alone. There are neighbors, yes, good people living a mile away in one direction or two miles in the other, but what is she to do? Pack her dying baby in blankets and trundle off into the frozen darkness?

No, there is nothing to do but rock. And pray. Always there's the praying.

She can't help it. In England, as a girl, she'd always prayed, prayed so much her father said she was addled, called her Saint Matilda. Then she prayed her way right to the Mormons and their exhilarating God of answered conversations—a God who talks right back—and her father wasn't teasing anymore when he called her a lunatic, mad, as sorry a creation as he'd ever made, and ordered her straightway out of the house. And so she prayed once more and was taken in by sympathetic Saints. She met a man—her quiet, sensible husband—and together they prayed themselves onto a ship and away from England to a wide frightening place called America, which they commenced to walk across together until they stopped, exhausted and full of prayer, in Salt Lake City, in Zion, and beseeched their Heavenly Father for rest.

It was in Salt Lake City she lost her fourth baby, the redheaded boy who resembled her father. On the day of the baby's burial she stood with her feet sinking low in the soft dirt dug for his grave and told God good-bye. *Farewell*, she said. *You have taken everything, and you don't keep your promises.* Three times previously she had prayed for her babies' lives—with faith, she was sure of it, mighty faith—and three times he had answered her no, and three times she had wept in anguish but had also said words like, "God's will be done," and "Soon we'll meet again in heaven." She knelt beside her bed in prayer on the nights she'd buried all three of those babies and pleaded with God, *No more*, hopeful that he would hear her.

When her fourth child died, she decided that God had not been listening, after all. Perhaps he had disappeared entirely. God was nowhere to be found, but she couldn't keep children out of her line of vision. Everywhere she looked, she saw them: children running and shouting and pulling on their mothers' sleeves, children climbing to the tops of trees without slipping, diving into deep water without drowning. Even worse, she saw the sick children who'd been healed, the ones who tottered out of their houses ashen and shaky after being shut up contagious with illness. Healed! Miracle children! All around her, it seemed, children with the mark of God's infinite grace and mercy fixed forever on their countenances, rushing—full of life and chosen—right into their mothers' arms.

"No longer," she told her husband the night of her son's funeral, when he knelt beside their bed to pray. She lay stiff and straight, the quilt tucked up tight under her arms. He didn't say a word, just nodded one short nod and said a prayer himself, then slid in bed beside her.

She kept her silence with God for many months. Then one summer day while feeding chickens in the yard, her thoughts wandered; she found herself talking to God as she once had, telling him her troubles in her mind. She spoke to God in an ordinary way, thinking things like, *Lord, this hen is not a good laying hen, I could use your blessing on this hen.* Suddenly she realized to whom her mind had turned. *What have I done?* she thought. *How can I be speaking to him again, so easily, as if nothing has happened between us?* But she found she couldn't stop herself. She sat straight down on the ground in her skirts and said everything she had to say to him, telling all the ways he'd deserted her, how she felt hollowed out by tribulation, that she didn't understand what more could be expected of her. She dug her fingers deep into the dirt and sobbed. She raised her head and opened her eyes against the glaring blue sky and said out loud, her voice ringing up to heaven, "I've had all I can bear."

And that's the prayer she prays as she rocks, over and over, as insistent as the Indian chants she hears sometimes, throbbing down from the mountains at night. *I've had all I can bear.* She knows that he can hear her. She doesn't know if he agrees.

The sun comes up huge and soft, filling the room with a hazy yellow light. Tildy stops rocking and her eyes are closed, not in sleep, but in an exhausted fight against it. Christina pants in Tildy's arms, her fever unbroken.

A gust of cold air rises up and over Tildy's body, and she feels the hair on her arms prick up. She breathes the taste of winter into her mouth. Before opening her eyes she thinks, *Death has come, and I know it now so well, I recognize it on my skin and taste it on my tongue.*

But she is wrong. As soon as her eyes open, she sees her front door blown ajar. A dusting of snow skims across the floor and over her feet. She rises for the first time in hours to go to the door, aching, her hot baby clutched to her chest.

When she sees him, she's too frightened to release the scream from her throat.

Standing in the corner by the kitchen table is a man. He is not a large man—maybe as tall as Tildy herself—but his hair is terrifying, bright white and blown up on its ends. He stands with his palms open, facing her as if in surrender. "I mean you no harm," he says, and his voice is tranquil and low. He looks directly into Tildy's face. His eyes are the darkest brown, the deepest eyes Tildy has ever seen, and his skin is as smooth as a boy's. But he is not a young man, she can tell, not only from his hair but from his look of weary calm.

"I just called to see your sick baby," he says.

Tildy pulls Christina in closer. *I will not give this baby up to death,* she thinks. But then she brings her eyes level with the eyes of the white-haired man and studies them evenly, and she knows he is not death. He is the opposite of death.

"She's a very sick baby," Tildy says.

"I know," says the man. He moves toward the baby and Tildy stays where she is, Christina cradled tight in her arms. The man reaches out his hand and tests her fever, touching his fingertips to the baby's forehead, cupping his palm against her cheek.

"Sister Palmer, you have had a lot of trouble," he says. He won't take his eyes from her face, and she can feel his warm breath on her skin. "Your babies have been taken from you. But you have been faithful through it all, and God will bless you. Your little girl will get well and will marry and have a large family. She will be a leader among women. She will lead as long a life as she desires."

"Yes, yes she will," Tildy says, her voice certain, unwavering. The man folds his hands over the top of Christina's tiny head, covering her brow and her skull and the tops of her ears. He whispers a blessing, says "Christina, be healed," then he takes his hands off her head and steps back. Tildy folds the baby in close to her body and kisses the top of her head and her cheeks and her neck, kisses all the skin she can find, skin still damp with sweat and warm with the fever she now knows will break. She closes her eyes and breathes in the smell of her baby: clean, sweet, alive.

"Peace be unto this house," the man says. He stands in her open doorway, the cold air swirling past him.

"Thank you," Tildy says, and he nods at her and smiles. Then he is gone.

Tildy studies Christina's face, the shape of her nose, the height of her forehead, the line of her tiny jaw and chin. She feels as if she's known Christina always: who she was and who she is and who she will be. "You get to stay here, with me," Tildy says. The baby's sleep seems smoother already. Soon Tildy will watch her wide eyes open.

She goes to the front door and steps out into the daylight. She doesn't wonder who the man is, where he came from, or where he has gone. Squinting out into the winter sun, she is not surprised to find herself alone. There is no one around for miles. Just the unbroken snow, the glaring whiteness of it stretching away from her, crisp and glittering and calm. Her warm breath turns to vapor in the cold. It mingles with her daughter's, and rises.

Kyle—2000

CB

MISSION CALL

Kyle opens the mailbox and there it is, balancing on top of the pile of bills and coupons and junk mail. A gleaming white envelope with the familiar boxy logo: The Church of Jesus Christ of Latter-day Saints.

Every day for the last month he has rushed home from work and yanked back the mailbox door on its creaky hinges. Every day he's rifled through the letters with shaky hands, his heart pumping, frantically scanning the return addresses in the upper left-hand corner and then, not finding his mission call, going back through them again, slower, careful not to miss it. Two other guys he knows put in their papers the same time he did, and they got their calls weeks ago. "Maybe yours got lost in the mail," people have been joking. "Maybe the Prophet's having second thoughts about you." Kyle would try to laugh but couldn't, too sick with fear that perhaps they were right. Perhaps the call would never come. He'd wanted to contact the Church Office Building and ask somebody in charge. He even flipped through the white pages once, running his finger down the hundreds of entries under "Church of Jesus Christ of Latter-day Saints," but he wasn't able to find any phone number that seemed right. His girl-friend, Beth, tried to calm him down. "Be patient," she told him. "It's just more time that we can be together." But he couldn't be patient. He felt like he did back in high school running track, up on the balls of his feet at the starting line, tense and ready any instant to shoot forward into the future.

And now he holds the call in his hands, surprised by how light-weight it seems. Shouldn't it be heavier, he thinks, more substantial, with the next two years of his life contained inside it? Again he feels the fear sweep over him. What if it's like college, the fat letters to those who'd been accepted, the skinny ones to those who weren't quite worthy? *Thank you for your desire to serve*, the letter could say, *but through process of revelation we have discerned your impure thoughts, your selfish appetites, your lackadaisical attitudes and meager knowledge of the scriptures.* What if? He's never heard of such a thing, though. Surely somebody would have brought it up by now.

He bangs inside the front door, the screen snapping shut behind him, and yells for his mother.

"Mom! It came!"

Her car's parked in the driveway, and he can hear the TV laugh track coming from her upstairs bedroom. She's home.

"Mom!" he shouts. Nothing.

He takes the stairs two at a time and flings open her door. Her drapes are drawn; the lights are off. Only the flicker of the television screen helps him see her, bunched up under her covers, an arm flung across her forehead.

"Quiet," she moans. "My head."

It's always her head. Her head or her gut. He sits on the edge of the bed beside her, the springs squeaking under his weight.

"It came," he says.

"What are you talking about?" she mumbles, turning her face away from him.

"My mission call. It's here. It came."

"Oh no," she groans into her pillow. "Already?"

"Come on, Mom. At least try. Be a little happy for me."

"I give my life to that church and what do they do? They take you away. Snatch a mother's only child, the only person she has in the wide world, and that's religion? That's the thanks I get?"

Kyle sighs. He won't have this conversation. But it's not his mother he wants to share the news with anyway, it's Beth and the Palmers. Beth's dad has been almost as anxious as Kyle—"Has it come yet? What's the holdup?"—and Beth's mom Alicia likes to call Kyle her surrogate missionary. With three girls in the family, two of them married and the last one (hopefully) more likely to be interested in a wedding than a mission once she turns twenty-one, Alicia says her chances of being a missionary mom are slim. Kyle's happy to play the part.

"But you're coming tonight, right? To the Palmers'? They said the day it comes, no matter the day, they want to invite everybody over. Have pie. Open it together."

"Glad to hear your mother's invited to such a soiree." She fumbles at the nightstand, knocking bottles of pills to the floor. "Damn it. Kyle? Help your mother, please. Give your mother a hand."

He picks up the pill bottles. "Which one you want?"

"Want? How about need? Fancy get-togethers. Spur of the moment. I need two of the blue ones. And a white. I'd like to be presentable."

He pops open the lids, counts out the pills.

"I'll need some time to freshen up," she says, then points the remote at the television, changing channels.

Kyle decides to drive to the Palmers' and tell them in person that the call came. He wants to see the looks on their faces. He turns into the driveway and sees Beth's mom outside pulling weeds.

"Hey you!" she yells.

Kyle climbs out of his car and waves the call high over his head, flashing the white envelope in the sun.

Alicia's eyebrows jump, her mouth opens wide. "Could it be?"

she says, beaming, thrilled.

Kyle nods, waves the call again in the air. "It is! The day has arrived!"

Alicia wipes her hands on her jeans then cups them around her mouth. "Beth!" she yells. "Get out here. Hurry up!"

The front door opens and Beth steps onto the porch. She looks at her mother's face, then Kyle's, and before anyone has a chance to tell her, her expression changes.

"This is it," she says. "Right? Today's the day?"

Kyle nods his head.

"I can't believe it. Already?" She's motionless, pale.

"What do you mean, already? It's the day we've been waiting for. Don't just stand there on the porch. Come here," he says, opening his arms wide. "You've got to be happy for me. It's your job. Support your missionary and all that."

She comes to him and wraps her arms around his waist, squeezing him tight. Her heart knocks against his chest. She tilts her head up and kisses him, quick.

"Oh," she says. "Whoops. I can still kiss you, right?"

"Come on, Bets, it's just the call. I'm not a missionary yet."

"So I can kiss you all I want, then?"

"Yoo hoo," Alicia says. "Mom in vicinity."

Kyle grins at Alicia over his shoulder. "Sorry to tell you, but I've been kissing your daughter for years."

"But not for much longer," Alicia says. "Twenty-four months of kisslessness."

"For me at least. Your daughter I'm not so sure about."

"Come on, now. Where's the trust?" Beth looks up into his face, her eyebrows raised in exaggerated innocence.

"Don't give me that look," he says. "I know your power. One glance and guys drop to your feet and worship."

"The only worshipping I'll be doing with other guys for the next two years is at church. Now forget it, will you?"

"Whatever you say."

"And just because you're on a mission doesn't mean you don't have to watch yourself too, buddy. All these single girls will take one look at you and turn Mormon before they know what hit them. They'll have little Elder Hewitt fan clubs."

"I'm just an innocent Utah boy, only kissed one girl in my life. And I intend to keep it that way." He kisses her again, longer this time.

"Enough!" Alicia says. "Inside, both of you. There's a pie to be made."

Kyle met Beth when he was fifteen, the age when he'd surprised himself by turning handsome. He never knew his father, and his mother's features had turned so uniformly flaccid and pale by the time he was old enough to study them that he never expected his own physical body to be anything but a means to get him from one place to another. But puberty hit him full-on the end of ninth grade, filling in his pectorals, sculpting the muscles in his back, throwing his voice down to a register that made teenaged girls think he knew things he didn't. They would send him notes in class ("I know somebody who thinks you're HOT!" "Hey gorgeous!"). He felt paralyzed by these notes, and confused, not knowing whether he was expected to write back, and if so, what he should say. So he ignored them.

Beth never sent him any notes. She sat two rows to the left of him in second period health, and one day late in fall, their teacher, Mr. Flannigan, called both of them up to the front of the class to demonstrate the Heimlich maneuver. Kyle knew her name: she was cute, funny, popular. A little intimidating. When she wrapped her arms around him from behind and balled her fists up against his ribcage, it seemed to Kyle the exercise was somehow inappropriate. Couldn't Mr. Flannigan get in trouble for making them do this sort of thing? He felt her breasts, pressing hard against his back. She jerked up and into his chest with such ferocity he thought his heart might give. Mr. Flannigan complimented her on her good form.

On the way back to their seats she beamed at him.

"If you ever need somebody to save your life, you know where to find her," she said.

The boldness of her proposition hit him in his gut and spread, liquid and thrilling, to the bottoms of his feet, the tips of his fingers. He did need somebody to save him. He saw right away she wasn't like those other girls, silly types, most of them, afraid even to look him in the eye. Beth was different, he could tell. Confident and easy with herself. At that moment she seemed the most impressive girl he'd ever met.

Mr. Flannigan announced a pop quiz, and when Kyle reached down to put his book away, his hands were shaking so badly he could hardly unzip his backpack. All during the quiz he kept his head low, his eyes fixed on his own hand scribbling answers to Mr. Flannigan's questions. But he could feel Beth's gaze on him, warm, as if he'd turned one side of his face to the sun.

"Time's up," Mr. Flannigan said. "Pass your papers one to the left."

Kyle had to turn toward her and there she was, watching him, her eyes round and blue and unafraid. She smiled. And that was it. Kyle was all hers.

For the longest time they couldn't go on real dates because neither one of them was sixteen. Not that Kyle's mother would stand in his way. "Do what you want," she'd been telling him for years. "So long as you don't make a mess for me to clean up." But Kyle didn't want to date until he was sixteen because good Mormon kids knew they shouldn't. His mom didn't go to church much, mainly when she needed extra groceries from the bishops' storehouse, but Kyle went every week. Got himself up, showered, dressed, tucked his scriptures under his arm and headed out. At church, life made sense to him. He was reminded that God had a plan, that people suffered for a reason, that if you were righteous and hardworking and kept the commandments, you'd be blessed. And his friends were there, his church leaders. One or two nights a month a different family in the ward would have him over, feed him dinner, and let him hang out.

He made the ward members feel good about themselves, he knew. A boy to guide to heaven! But Kyle didn't worry about their motives. He wanted guiding. It worked out well for everybody.

But Beth's parents were strict about not dating till sixteen. When Kyle walked into their house for the first time he could tell they would be: a cross-stitched sampler hanging in the entry that said, "My Family is Forever"; a picture of President Benson stuck to the fridge with a magnet; a ceramic temple on the fireplace mantle. Beth told her parents Kyle was her study partner.

When he started showing up at their door a few times a week, Beth's mom, Alicia, would joke with him. "You two are going to be the smartest sophomores in the whole dang school," she said.

He knew she suspected the real story, but he was good at winning moms over. He'd been doing it since he was five, wriggling his way into other families' homes.

"Let me do that," he said when Alicia came struggling in the door with her groceries. He noticed little touches around the house. "Did you arrange those flowers yourself?" he asked. Or he gave compliments. "Your pantry is so organized!" "You look great today! Red is your color."

"Be careful," Beth teased him. "My mom's falling in love."

But it was Kyle who'd fallen in love, fallen hard and fast, with the singular ferocity of a lonely teenaged boy. In love with Beth, with her family, her life. *Finally*, he thought, *maybe this is the place for me, a warm place I can call home.*

By seven o'clock, the pie is ready and the family sits waiting to open the call. Nathan, Alicia, and Beth are there, of course, but Grandma Tess has shown up too, and Tina's come with little Ava.

"Where's Curtis?" Kyle asks her. Tina and her husband moved up to Salt Lake from Cedar City last year in search of a better job. Kyle likes Curtis—a quiet guy, but nice, and not LDS, so the family loves it when he's around for events like this just in case a little

Mormon dust rubs off on him—but Kyle hasn't seen him much lately.

Tina waves her hand in the air. "Who knows," she says. "Outer Mongolia for all I care."

Alicia sends Tina a hard look, then glances to Grandma Tess and back to Tina again. Tina takes a deep breath.

"Working, I mean," she says loudly, in Grandma's direction. "He's *working*."

Kyle feels for Tina—her shotgun marriage, her struggles to make ends meet. He wonders if she's uncomfortable at times like these, seeing the happiness that comes when a person does what's right and follows the rules. He knows her mother holds Beth up as an example: a good girl and a *happy* girl, making smart choices, dating a good Mormon guy, setting herself up for an easier life than Tina has created, a life where Heavenly Father can bless her better.

Nathan walks into the room, holding the phone in the air. "We've got another surprise guest," he says. "It's Marnie!"

"Hey, Marnie!" everybody yells, and Nathan puts the phone to his ear and says, "Everybody says hey!"

Beth's oldest sister Marnie moved to Minnesota last year, after marrying some rich MBA student she met at a singles' dance, a guy who's originally from Minneapolis. Mike is his name. Kyle tries to like him, but it's hard. He comes off so pompous sometimes. For instance, there was the no-class way Mike's family paid for a fancy wedding reception at the Joseph Smith Memorial Building when it should have been Alicia's deal. The mother of the bride! He'd talked to Alicia at length about the snub, how she'd planned to decorate the cultural hall, how her friends were all lined up to work in the kitchen—she'd even made black-and-white serving aprons for the Young Women to wear—and in sweeps Mike's mother wearing her little designer dress and spiky-heeled shoes, acting like *she* was the one doing the favor, paying for the reception Alicia didn't even want. But Alicia had been gracious, thanking her profusely, never accepting anybody's compliments about how well the reception had gone. ("I'm afraid you'll have to thank Mike's mother for that," she'd say. "Folks like us don't pull off such fancy events without help.") But Kyle told Mike in no uncertain terms how lucky he was to marry into the family. At the wedding, he said, "You better be good to the Palmers, or you'll have me to answer to," then punched him playfully, but a little hard, in the arm.

"Marnie might have to hang on a few minutes, still," Kyle says to Nathan. "I don't want to open it without my mom here."

Kyle had asked his mother to be to the Palmers' by 7:00 and here it is 7:40. The pie is already long gone. They've even played the guess-the-mission-call game: each person sticks a colored pin in a world map hanging on the wall to mark his pick for where Kyle will go, and the closest guess wins a giant Hershey bar with almonds. Nathan picked Peru because he went there, back in the sixties; Tina picked Timbuktu, to be funny; Alicia picked Italy since it's a place she's always dreamed of visiting; and Beth picked Florida because it's warm and pretty and (most importantly) in the U.S., so the mail service will be quick. Kyle picked Russia since—and he hasn't told anyone this—in his heart of hearts, he's sure the Lord is going to send him to a choice place, a place where the gospel is new and the work is hard and only the most valiant can meet the challenges.

"So where is your mother working these days?" Grandma Tess asks. Kyle figures she's only trying to be polite, but he hates questions like these. "She's teaching economics at the U!" he wants to be able to say. "She's curing cancer! Making movies!"

"She's still assistant manager at the Circle K," he says. "Working nights, usually. She likes the night shift. So she doesn't miss her TV shows, I guess."

"Is she still doing Amway as well?"

Kyle cringes. Last year his mother had been obsessed with Amway. She quoted him the testimonials, showed him all the glossy pictures in the brochure. "A hundred thousand a year," she said. "And you make your own hours!" She even called Alicia up and invited herself to the Palmers' house to give the Amway pitch. Kyle

147

had to sit through the whole agonizing night with Beth, Nathan, Grandma Tess, and Alicia listening to his mother rattle on about discount detergents and the wisdom of buying in bulk.

"Not so much anymore. It didn't exactly turn out like she thought."

"Yes, well," Grandma Tess says. "It's a difficult thing, making ends meet for your family. Especially all alone. She's doing her best, I'm sure."

The doorbell rings. From his seat in the living room, Kyle can see his mother—finally—peering through the glass. He motions to her with his hand.

"Come in, Mom," he yells. "The door's open."

She's dressed in her Sunday clothes: skirt, nylons, old white pumps with scuffed up heels. Her make-up looks as if she's applied it in the dark. The blue of her eye shadow extends up into her eyebrows and, when she smiles, he sees a smudge of pink lipstick staining her front tooth.

"Hope I haven't held up the party," she says. "Just a busy day, lots to do. Cleaning the house, working extra shifts. It's all just, well, there's so much, you know. To be done. But my boy!" She claps her hands. "My little man. You've saved that seat for me?"

She points to the wedge of space between Kyle and Beth on the loveseat.

"Sure," Beth says, patting it. "Right here." She and Kyle move away from each other and smash their bodies into either side of the couch. Kyle's mother comes toward them, tottering just slightly in her heels. Kyle knows her glassy eyes, her wobbly gait. He recognizes that she probably didn't stop at three pills, even four or five or six. He's never said a word to the Palmers—even to Beth—about all the medication, and he prays they don't recognize the signs. How would they? Sure, Tina drank in high school, going to parties and all that, but have they ever seen a grown-up acting like this and known what to blame it on? Alicia's told him, "Your mother—she's a character," which is fine for her to say. Let her think his mother's strange, a little loopy; Alicia can believe that being unpredictable and odd is just an unchangeable part of his mother's personality. She's a *character*, behaving as she does because God made her that way. She squeezes in beside him.

"So is it time?" Alicia asks. "You want to open it?"

"Wait!" Kyle's mother says. "The map. I haven't had my turn."

She plants her hand on Kyle's thigh and heaves herself up. "Don't want the mother left out, now do you?"

"Sorry, Louise," Nathan says. "Would you like to choose a pin?" He hands her the plastic box of pins and she rifles through it, taking her time.

"I want to find a yellow," she says. "A lucky color. Sunshiny. Ah! There's one." She takes her pin and walks to the map and peers at it. "Now where's the Middle East? It's so small, that part of the world. Smashed in there by Europe, I never know where I'm looking."

"But Mom, there's not . . ."

"Did I tell you all about my dream? The Holy Land. When Kyle was just a little boy, I'd been pretty sick, pretty tired of it all, and the Lord came to me in a dream. Said, 'Your son will by my emissary in the Holy Land.' Or something like that. Ah ha!" She sticks her pin into the map. "There we go. Jerusalem. So tiny! But I know it. That's where he's going, I feel it in my bones."

Kyle knows there isn't a mission in Jerusalem. Too dangerous, or there's a law against it or some such reason. "Mom," he says, "There isn't . . ."

Nathan interrupts him. "Good choice, Louise. All sorts of places in the world to get sent."

"Well I know my son," she says, heading back to her place in the couch. "The Lord's got big plans for him." She squeezes his knee.

"So now can we open it?" Beth asks. "I'm dying here."

"*You're* dying," Kyle says, and takes a deep breath. "All right then. Drum roll, please." The room is silent, everyone watching the envelope in Kyle's lap. This is one of those moments, he thinks, like a wedding or the birth of a child might be, a time your brain slows down and you try to force it to record each passing second in freeze-frame: now you're putting your finger inside the envelope; now you're sliding along the width of it, listening to it tear; now you're reaching in and pulling out a bundle of papers, neatly folded in half; now you're unfolding them, seeing the church logo, seeing your name, Elder Kyle Hewitt, your mind thinking Russia, thinking Hong Kong, thinking Serbia or Panama or . . .

"Omaha," he says. "Nebraska." There it is, in black and white. English speaking (of course, English speaking) and he feels the vastness of the place already, settling under his skin. The expanse of it, the long emptiness, the color, even, a barely perceptible yellow sinking almost into beige. Nebraska. Kyle and his mother and the Palmers are still.

"Well now," Alicia says, breaking the silence. "Omaha. A lovely place. I drove through it once, I think, as a child. Lots of corn."

"Lots of corn? That's the best thing you can think to tell him? Come on, Mom," Tina shoots back. Kyle can always count on Tina to say what needs to be said. "At least you won't have to eat giant rats or anything, like some guy I know who went to Bolivia. Or learn Chinese. Spend half your mission with a headache trying to figure out what everybody's saying."

Kyle looks up, tries to smile. "Definitely," he says. "All positives. And corn is good. Nothing against corn."

Beth squeezes his hand. "I'm just glad you won't be far away. Or in danger. And you won't have to give up Taco Bell."

"True," he says. "Yep."

He looks over at his mother. Her face and neck are mottled red, her lips are pursed. He can hear her breath coming hard out her nose, angry. Please, Mom, he thinks. Don't do it.

"What a load of crap," she says.

The Palmers turn their heads simultaneously to gape at her. Tina, even, looks surprised.

"That's the stupidest thing I ever heard," she hisses. "Nebraska? Give me a break. Do they know what kind of boy they've got here?

150

How good he is? You don't send kids like this to Nebraska. You send him overseas, at least. Teach him a language. They think they're going to take him away from me for two years so he can go to *Nebraska*?"

"Mom," Kyle says, "It's okay. It's not like they send all the rejects to the states or something. Remember Corey Hunt? He was seminary president and he went to Texas."

"Spanish speaking," Beth says.

"You're not helping," Kyle says, a little sharp. He can feel the heat in his face, his body trembling. He thinks his mother's right. She's right! How stupid of him to believe the Lord would send him someplace special. He hasn't told a soul about the prayers he's been praying these last few months. He thought he'd been so connected, almost able to hear the spirit whispering *Prepare yourself, you are a chosen son.* But it's Nebraska. Of course, Nebraska.

"Now, Louise," Nathan says, "there's nothing shameful about a stateside mission. For heaven's sake! It's the same gospel wherever you go, God's same children all over the world. I assure you that it's no kind of indication of a person's character whether or not he goes foreign."

"And you're the expert in this because . . . ?" The question hangs in the room, unanswered. "Well, my boy, I say you just mail that thing back to the Church and tell them politely, thank you very much but no, try again, please."

"I'm not sending it back, Mom," Kyle says quietly, barely audible, looking down at his shoes.

"Why not? It's a travesty, a ridiculous travesty. Two years wandering around in some cornfield. I don't think so!"

Kyle closes his eyes. He can feel his heart churning in his chest, pushing blood into his ears, his face, his neck. He turns toward his mother and sees her sallow skin, the crimson rouge ground into her pores, the folds of fat along her neck.

"Nobody here wants to listen to you," Kyle says tightly. "Not me, not them. Can't you see it?"

Everyone turns to Kyle's mother, whose face has gone white, save for two bright red spots coloring her cheeks.

"Well, now. That was uncalled for," she says. Her voice trembles slightly. "I think I deserve an apology."

"I'm not apologizing," Kyle says, his volume rising. "I've had it. Do you know what they think of you?" He flings his arm out at the Palmers. "They think you're insane. Everybody does!"

His mother brings both hands to her mouth.

"Oh, Louise," Alicia says. "I'm sure he didn't . . . you have to understand. It's an emotional time, an emotional day."

Kyle's mother turns to her, glaring, her eyes narrow and searing. "And who do you think you are? His mother or something?"

"No, I . . ." Alicia stumbles. "Not at all, I just . . ."

"You think it's fun being me? Being us? My whole life long it's been the two of us, Kyle and me, and we've had our struggles, for sure. Rough patches. But he's always been mine. *My* child. And a good boy too, and I raised him. Not you." She stands and points a shaky finger around the room. "All of you think you're doing him some kind of favor, rescuing him. From what? From his real life, from the person he is? Well praise be the Palmers. They can take a boy from his mother and teach him to hate her."

"We never," Nathan says. "Trust me, Louise, it was never our intention . . ."

She raises her palm. "Enough. I've had enough." She strides across the living room, her heels clapping against the hardwood floor. "And if the son I know happens to reappear, tell him I'll be waiting for him. At home. *His* home."

The slam of the front door rings through the house, then silence. Kyle stands, letting his mission papers fall from his lap and onto the floor. He steps over them clumsily, catching a paper under his shoe and kicking it aside. Then he rushes out the back door.

Kyle stands on the back porch watching the road snaking out of the Palmers' neighborhood. His mother's car has left—he saw it go

—but he feels as though he's cosmically wedded to this exact spot in the Palmers' backyard, unable to get in his car and drive after his mother, unable to return inside to Beth and her family. Alone, outside, immobile, the sky above him sinking deeper into black. He's facing east. Toward Nebraska.

"Heavenly Father," he whispers.

The night is silent and still. No sighing trees, no whisper of wind.

"Help me."

Behind him, the door unlatches. He feels a hand on his shoulder. Nathan. Kyle doesn't turn to look at him, doesn't speak, and Nathan joins him in the silence. It's a warm evening. The stars are out, winking and glistening, alive. For a few minutes they stand together and watch the night.

"I'm okay," Kyle says. "I'm good."

"I know you are."

"Everything's going to be all right."

"Just trust that," Nathan says. "Believe it. It's true."

Kyle closes his eyes, repeats the prayer in his mind. *Help me.*

"You ready to head back in?" Nathan asks. "The family's waiting for you. They're anxious to celebrate."

"Sure," he says. "I can't stay out here forever, now can I?"

"You can't," Nathan says. "There are folks in Nebraska waiting. Just for you."

Marnie—2003

cs

BIRTHDAY

I've told Mike I don't care if it's a boy or a girl. That's what I've said to everybody. "Just so long as it's healthy," I say, or "I wouldn't know what to do with a girl." Which is a lie. I would know what to do with a girl: buy her dresses, braid her hair, teach her to sing. I already have her name picked out. Christina. A family name. Mike wasn't sure about the name at first—it is Tina's name, after all, and Aunt Christy's name too—but I told him we'd call her Christina and nothing else. No nicknames, nothing short. It's a beautiful name, I think.

When I called my mother this morning to tell her we were headed to the hospital she said, "I can't wait to meet our little girl!"

"Don't be so sure it's a girl, Mom."

"Grandmas can tell," she said. "If you're not going to take advantage of the ultrasound, grandmas are the next best thing."

My mom hates that I didn't find out the baby's sex. "Why prolong the agony?" she said. As the mother of all girls, she's familiar with this particular kind of anticipation. She never had a son. And now, as the mother of two boys myself, I might find with number three that I'll never have a daughter.

I'd have a big family if I could, keep on going if this one's a boy. But this baby will be my last. Mike doesn't want any more. He's sure of it. He's from a big Mormon family and tells me that, in his experience, if there are too many kids in the house you're liable to lose your focus, get overwhelmed, and before you know it one or more of them has gone off the deep end. When I tried to argue with him he reminded me how unfair it would be to bring a child into the world if both parents weren't a hundred percent on board.

Right now I'm in my hospital bed and Mike is in the chair beside me, sleeping. I've been in labor fourteen hours and haven't felt a lick of it. I'm one week overdue; when they brought me in to induce me, I was already dilated to a four, so I talked them into hooking me up to the Pitocin and giving me an epidural at the same time. I've been wide awake and waiting for half a day now, and I know if I was smart I'd get some rest while I still can. But I'm afraid if I sleep, my uterus will sleep with me. I want to get this baby out. Meet her.

"You're not going to be disappointed if it's a boy, then?" people ask me.

"Of course not!" I answer. "I'll take whatever God sends me."

Although I did tell God last night, I'll take what you send me, but please send me a girl. Right after saying that prayer I fell asleep and had a dream about her. She was wearing a pair of plaid overalls, and her hair was dark brown and straight with bangs cut to frame her face. She looked like me when I was little. When I woke up this morning I was so sure she was my daughter I was afraid to say anything to Mike, for fear she wouldn't come true.

I hear the door open, and the night nurse comes in to check my progress. She puts her hand inside me, testing the width of my cervix with her fingers. I've been dilated to a six now for hours. Stuck.

"This is why I tell them to wait until you're good and going before they give the epidural," she says, and looks down at me accusingly. I wonder about night nurses. What's happened in their lives to send them to work while everyone else is sleeping?

"Do you have any children?" I ask her. She's older. Fifty, maybe. She isn't wearing a ring.

"Three," she says. She seems surprised that I've asked her a personal question. I'm sure night nurses don't get talked to much.

"Boys? Girls?"

"Three boys," she says. "Used to be lots of excitement at my house."

"I have two boys."

She offers up a small smile. "And will this make it three?"

"I don't know yet. It's going to be a surprise."

"You want a girl, I bet," she says. "I did. Had a wedding dress I wanted to pass down. Had some old dolls."

The night nurse has strong cheekbones and full lips. She must have been pretty once. If she'd had a daughter, right now she would have been in her late teens or early twenties. The beautiful years. She could remind her mother what she looked like when she was young.

"Do you ever wish you had a girl?" I ask.

"Sometimes. My boys are grown now. Gone. I can't help but think if I had a daughter she would have stuck around." She walks over to the heart rate monitor and checks the tape. "You're looking fine. Just try to relax. That can help things to move along. Maybe sleep a little."

"I'll try," I say. She leaves and I close my eyes. A wave of exhaustion rolls through me, and I think maybe a little rest might do me good. I realize that the muscles in my body are tight: my jaw is clenched, my shoulders are bunched. I concentrate on releasing and letting go.

While I'm sleeping I dream again of the brown-haired girl. This time she's wearing my wedding gown.

"Where did you get that dress?" I ask her. I don't have it to give to her because I didn't buy my wedding dress; I rented it. It was the only way I could afford one nice enough that I wouldn't be embarrassed in front of Mike's parents.

"I stole it," she says. "I'm a thief."

She looks to be only three or four years old, but her eyes are wise and cutting.

"No, no you're not. You're a good girl. You're a nice girl." My heart is racing. I need to get the dress off her and return it to the rightful owner. I try to undo the buttons but there are so many of them, and they're so tiny. My fingers keep slipping.

"You want this dress?" she says. "Fine. Take it."

She disappears. The dress puddles to the floor.

When I wake up I feel pressure.

"Mike," I say, shaking his shoulder. "It's time. Get the nurse."

He awakens in the chair with a start. A crease runs the length of his face, and his blonde hair is tousled and wild. He is what my boys will look like thirty years from now. Both of them are Iversons in every way: tall, fair, athletic, self-assured. Sometimes Mike jokes that I'm nothing but an incubator.

"You're sure?" he asks.

I feel the undeniable heaviness between my legs.

"Positive," I say. "Get her quick."

I look over at the heart monitor and see the baby's rate is in the eighties. I read a lot of baby books and I know this isn't good.

"Mike!" I yell. He's out in the hall. Where are the nurses? The doctors? Why did I allow myself to fall asleep? The pressure is insistent. I imagine the baby sliding out from inside me and onto the bed with no one to catch her.

"Mike!"

He races into the room with the night nurse. She whips back my blanket and reaches in to feel how close the baby is to crowning.

"He's almost here. But you have to concentrate, now. Push. His heart rate's a little low, so let's get him out."

"Where's the doctor?" Mike says. His face is colorless. "Get a doctor in here!"

"The doctor's coming as quick as he can," the night nurse says. Her voice is measured, calm but in a practiced way, as if she's used to talking like this in serious situations so she can keep patients from panicking. My epidural has worn off considerably and I can feel each contraction now, gripping my middle and ripping all the way down my thighs. I moan.

"Try to stay with me," the night nurse says. "Stay calm. Think about your pushing."

I push so hard my whole body trembles, so much I can feel the grit of my teeth as they grind.

"Harder," the nurse says. Her voice is clipped, sharp, demanding.

I gasp for breath. I look over at the monitor and see the baby's heart rate sliding, down, down, down.

"Push!" Mike says.

I bear down. I hear myself scream.

"Head's out," the night nurse says. "Good girl, good job."

"Is that the cord?" Mike stands at the foot of the bed, his eyes wide with terror. "Is that the thing around his neck? Is he breathing?"

The night nurse doesn't answer him. She looks right at me, trying to send me some strength with her eyes. "One more push," she tells me. "One more push and he's out."

I push so hard I see stars. Blackness starts at the edge of my vision and gathers. Then I hear Mike.

"It's a boy!" he shouts.

My whole world goes dark.

When I come to, Mike is beside me, brushing my hair back from my face. I hear a baby crying.

"Are you okay?" he asks. "Are you with me?"

I don't have the energy to speak. I nod. I want to see my baby.

"He's okay. He's crying. He came out a little blue, but he's pinking

159

up real quick. You did great, honey!" He kisses me on the cheek. "You did awesome!"

"It's a boy?" I whisper.

"He's beautiful," Mike says. "See? He looks just like the others."

The night nurse brings me my son wrapped in a plain white blanket and wearing a sky-blue cap. "He's a big one," she says. "Almost nine pounds. Takes after his dad, I can tell." She lays him in my arms.

I look at his face, swollen from birthing. Mike's right, he looks just like his brothers.

"What should we name him?" Mike asks.

"I don't know," I say. My mind is empty of names and I'm too tired to find them. "You decide."

It's morning and Mike has gone to his sister's house to pick up our boys. He's bringing them here to the hospital to meet their brother, who is sleeping in his bassinet beside me. Before Mike left, he opened the curtains so I could see outside. The winter sky shines vivid blue, alive with cold. In the courtyard I see a cardinal, red as blood, bright against the barren trees. A beautiful bird, one of my favorite birds of Minnesota. This one's a male, of course. The female is a dull reddish brown and harder to notice.

I pick up the phone and dial my mother. Mike called her right after the baby was born to make the announcement. I heard him say boy, nine pounds, looks just like his brothers. He held the phone to me but I shook my head. Too tired, I whispered. Now I listen as the phone rings back to Utah.

"Sweetie!" my mother says. She knows it's me right away; the Minnesota area code on the caller ID gives me away.

I start to cry. "I need you to be here," I say.

I can tell she doesn't know how to answer. I told her to wait, to come in two weeks when Mike goes back to work and I'll need the most help.

"Oh, Hon," she says. "Are you okay?"

I cry. I cradle the phone against my shoulder and sob.

"Do you want me to come now? Today? I can figure out a way, if you need me to." I hear her stop and pull in all her breath. "Is the baby okay?"

"He's fine," I say. "I'm looking at him right now. He's asleep."

She exhales. "Well you're just tired, honey. It's so hard, having a baby. The hardest thing you'll ever do."

"It wasn't very hard. I didn't feel much pain."

"You probably just need to sleep. Rest. Your body's been through a lot, even if you didn't feel it all."

I don't answer her. I take a few deep breaths. Maybe I should just tell her *Yes, yes, you're right—I'm just tired is all*, then say good-bye and hang up, because I'm not sure how to say what I called to tell her. That I don't know if I can love my baby the way I'm supposed to. That he's not who I thought he was going to be.

"So it's a boy," she says softly.

"It's a boy." I never told my mother about the daughter I imagined. Dreamed. Christina. I told her what I knew I should say, like I did with everyone else. And now I have to tell her I lied.

"Another boy," she says, and pauses. "It'll be okay."

I start to cry again, heavy sobs coming up from my chest. I hear the baby rousing in his bassinet.

My mom waits for my crying to diminish before she speaks. "Can I tell you a story?" she asks. "Because I know what you're feeling. When your sister, Beth, was born, I was certain she'd be a boy. I'd prayed about it. Fasted, even, although I knew I wasn't supposed to when I was pregnant. Your father wanted a boy so badly, and I wanted to be *done* so badly. I wasn't good at being pregnant or taking care of babies, like you are. It didn't come naturally to me. But I felt I couldn't ever be done until I gave your dad a son. He didn't say it in so many words, but the expectation was there, like it was my duty somehow. So Beth was born and I remember that first night in the hospital, trying to feed her, wincing every time she went to latch on and nurse, and I just sobbed and sobbed. I thought, *I can't do this again. And now I have to.* And there was no end in sight for me: I imagined myself with girl after girl after girl, pregnant forever but never with a son. And I was even angry at her. Little baby Beth. Can you believe it? This sweet baby, and a part of me wanted somebody to go to the nursery and switch her out with a boy. I never told anybody because I was so ashamed. After I had her I was quite depressed—postpartum had something to do with it, and I know that now—but I didn't want to talk to anybody. Not my friends. Not your father. Finally, when Beth was about six months old, your dad came to me and said, 'You've got to tell me what's wrong. I can't live this way.' And even though it terrified me, I told him the truth. I told him that I was done having babies—that I couldn't do it again, not ever—and I was sorry and I knew I was a terrible wife and a bad Mormon and he'd never have a son, but he needed to know the truth. And you know what? He understood, in his own way. Everything turned out fine. The way it was supposed to be. So, honey, I guess I just want to tell you it's okay to feel what you're feeling. I felt it. I know. But it will pass, and before you know it, you won't be able to imagine your family any other way than with him in it."

I've never heard this story before. None of us has. "Thank you, Mom," I say. I look over at my boy. He's awake now, eyes open and searching.

"Are you going to be okay?" she asks.

"I think so."

"You will be. I know. You're a better person than I was at your age, and I got through it. You will too."

"So you just told Dad?" I ask. "Told him what you really wanted, and he was okay with it?"

"He was. It took a little time, but he came around."

"Thank you for telling me that. I never knew. It means a lot."

The boys come, my visiting teacher, my neighbor. All with gifts: blue balloons, blue onesies, blue bibs.

"He's beautiful," they all tell me. "Perfect. And what's his name?"

"I don't know," I say. "Mike and I haven't quite decided."

When Mike's mother arrives she sits on the edge of my bed and peers into the baby's bassinet.

"No name yet, then," she says, her phrasing in the form of a statement, not a question. "To each her own, but I had all my babies' names picked out long before they were born. All eight times I had a girl name and a boy name, and all eight times the baby came out and I knew right away the name was perfect. Perhaps because I'd bonded with the baby already. Who knows?" She pats me absently on the leg. "But to each her own."

I have learned in five years of marriage not to take Mike's mother's comments too seriously, but it has been a difficult education. I remember when I flew to Minnesota to meet her and the rest of Mike's family after we'd gotten engaged, I was so sick with gut-wrenching fear and apprehension I almost threw up on the plane. Mike didn't get it.

"They're just my family," he told me. "They know I love you, and that's enough for them. You'll knock 'em out. No worries!"

But I was worried, and for good reason. Mike and I had known each other for all of three months when we got engaged. His family had scarcely heard a word about me before learning I was not just a nice girl he met at a singles' dance, but their golden boy's future wife. They'd never even seen my picture. But I'd seen plenty of pictures of them: flaxen-haired, beautiful, lean and tan and crisply tailored, all of them. All ten of them. And since Mike was the oldest boy, I was the first daughter-in-law for Mrs. Iverson to sink her expertly polished nails into.

But beyond the intimidation I felt from the wealth and attractiveness of Mike's family, I worried that Mike himself had made some kind of mistake in choosing me. I was stunned when he asked me out the first time; up until him, most of my short-lived relationships had been with shy, studious, slightly awkward types, and here was this beautiful man interested in *me* for some reason. He was rich, smart, a returned missionary almost done with his MBA.

163

Every girl at that singles' dance wanted him. Every girl. And he picked me.

Soon after we got engaged I worked up the nerve to ask him. "Why do you love me?" I said.

He didn't seem surprised by the question. "Lots of reasons," he told me. "First, you're not like other girls. Superficial and petty and all wrapped up in ridiculous stuff. I like that. And you're smart and fun to talk to. And most of all you're good-hearted. You're kind." He leaned over and kissed me on the head. "You'll make a wonderful mother."

I replayed that conversation in my mind for days before I figured out why it troubled me so much. Then I realized it was because he didn't tell me I was beautiful.

Mike's mother, however, is stunning. Even now, in her fifties, she's sharp enough to make men in the room take notice. When a male hospital worker walks in with a tray of food for my lunch, she turns and looks over her shoulder and gives him her most dazzling smile. I see him brighten immediately.

"Let me get out of your way," she says, scooting off my bed. "We grandmas tend to take up a lot of room."

"You can't be a grandma," he answers, taking her bait.

"Oh, but I am!" Her eyes dance. "Seven times over!"

The hospital worker shakes his head. "Lucky grandkids, I'm sure." He grins at her and puts my tray in front of me without glancing in my direction even once. As soon as he leaves, Mrs. Iverson starts poking at my food.

"For heaven's sake, what are they feeding you?" she asks. "Jell-O? Rolls?" She picks up my little plastic bottle of apple juice and peers at the label. "One hundred percent juice? Goodness." She sighs. "Sugar, sugar, sugar. And this is supposed to be an institution of health."

"It's actually not that bad here," I say. "The food, I mean. For a hospital."

She squeezes my knee under the blankets. "Well now is not the time to worry about sugar, I'm sure. You'll have plenty of time for that soon."

I breathe through my nose, slowly, deeply; then the baby starts fussing in his bassinet.

"He's hungry," I say. "I'd better, you know . . ."

One of the great things about Mrs. Iverson is how squeamish she gets about breastfeeding. The mother of eight, and never once did she even try it. I suspect she still finds it somewhat uncouth, but I count it as a good way to get her to leave a room.

"Of course, then, my dear. I'll leave you to it," she says. "Goodbye, little no name," she says, and leans down into the baby's bassinet and kisses him on the nose. "He looks just exactly like his father. Exactly!" she says proudly. "It's uncanny, almost."

"Mike's got strong genes."

"Yes, I suppose we Iversons do." She hoists her designer handbag over her shoulder and smoothes her skirt along her narrow hips. "Don't mess with the Iversons, I always say. Not even our DNA!"

I smile until I hear the door latch behind her.

After Mike gets back from dropping off the boys, a nurse comes in and hands us a stack of forms, one of which we need to turn in for the baby's birth certificate. She tells us to make our decision by morning or we'll have to deal with telling the government his name ourselves.

"I have an idea," Mike says. "I know you always wanted Christina, for a girl. Well what about Christopher? It's close to Christina. We could call him Chris. Chris Iverson. I like it. Sounds like a quarterback."

I hold the baby against my chest. He is warm and soft and heavy.

"No," I say. "Not Christopher." I take a breath. I swallow. "I'm saving Christina, still."

He looks at me, curious. "Saving it? For what?"

I can't help myself and look down at my bedspread. "For the next one," I answer.

"What?" he asks. I look up again and I see his face change, gathering inward, growing tighter, as the realization of what I've just told him moves across it. "But we decided. What are you talking about? I have my appointment. I'm going in for the procedure next month."

"I can't support you in that decision." My voice gains strength. It feels good to say this. Powerful. My body feels tingly and light, charged through with adrenaline. "I have a say. I have an opinion."

"Marnie." He sighs. "You're just tired. You're drained from having this baby. I know you wanted a girl, honey, but we could have a dozen babies and they could all end up boys."

"It's not about that," I say. And it's not. I look down at my son and there it is: love. I love this baby. Boy or girl, I love him, and having him was my choice. And I can choose to do it again.

"But what if you get pregnant again and it's another boy? What then? When does it ever stop?"

"I don't know, Mike. It stops when I feel like it should stop. I don't feel it yet."

"But we agreed. We made an agreement."

I lay my baby at the end of the bed and unwrap him from his swaddling. His thin legs are wound up against his body, and his tiny toes unfurl. He squirms, stretches, opens his mouth and yawns.

"I think this one looks like me. Can you see it?"

Mike doesn't look. "Marnie," he says. "Listen."

"Daniel," I say. "After the Old Testament prophet. The strong one, the one who faced the lions, the one who wouldn't back down. That's his name." I touch the baby's cheek with my finger. He turns toward it and opens his mouth like a bird, ready to eat.

"We'll talk about this later," Mike says.

My husband stands at the window, his posture straight, his chin raised high. He is just like my boys: stubborn, willful. It's hard to be married to a confident man, a smart man, a man you feel is just a little bit better than you deserve. It takes courage.

"Find a pen," I say. "Write the name down. It's perfect. It's him."

Mike turns around. Sees me. "Daniel," he repeats. "Are you sure?"

I fold my warm baby up against my skin. He latches on right away, easily, already knowing my body.

"I'm sure," I say. "Trust me. I know what I want."

I catch a blur of red move past the window behind him. The cardinal. I slide my eyes from Mike's face to the barren trees and snow and ice outside, and search, knowing she's somewhere nearby: the subtle bird, the girl. Cardinals mate for life. She's out there. It's a fact.

Mike follows my gaze, turns, and looks past his shoulder. "What are you looking for?"

I don't answer him. I smile.

Jimmy—2004

TINA'S WEDDING: PART TWO

So the thing that surprised me about these Utah weddings is how lots of times there's no dancing. Tina says sometimes there's dancing, but even then it's usually DJs, hardly ever live bands like mine. But Mormons aren't like those people from the movie *Footloose* who think dancing is sinful and all that. Tina's cousin is in her high school's dance company and I went to her concert with the Palmers a few months back, and I'm telling you, those Utah girls weren't shy about working it. I think the problem with Mormons dancing at weddings is there's not any booze, so the adults get all uptight about looking dumb in front of their kids. I mean, I think back to my own dad: alcohol-free, you'd be lucky to get him to snap his fingers, but after he got a few drinks in him he'd start moonwalking like Michael Jackson, which killed me to watch as a kid but I just had to deal with it.

At first Tina wanted to serve champagne at our wedding reception, but her mom said absolutely not. Mrs. Palmer said, "I'm paying for the thing, so I get to make the rules." It made Tina pretty mad, but I said, "Baby, she's got a point. And who's going to drink the champagne, anyway? A couple of your non-Mormon friends and my dad and his girlfriend and the three guys from my band and us?" But Tina was still all riled up about it and said, "Who cares what my mom's neighbors think, anyhow? It's my wedding and I should be able to drink champagne." So just to smooth things over I told her I'd buy us a bottle and hide it in with all the band's stuff and we'd crack it open when her mom wasn't looking. Good idea, no?

But I've gotta say, Tina's mom was pretty cool about the band. I could tell the thought of having a rock band at a wedding Mormons would be coming to made her nervous at first, but it wasn't just any band, it was my old band that I belonged to before I chased Tina up to Utah. My good friends. So Tina's mom told me, "I know it's special to you, Jimmy, and we want this to be your wedding too," which I told Tina was big of her mom to say, considering. Then Tina said, "Considering what?" She was still edgy about the whole champagne conversation and I wanted to kick myself for maybe making her mood even worse, so I just said, "Considering how your mom doesn't give in so easy." Tina seemed to take my word for it and left it at that, but what I meant was, considering this is your second marriage; considering you started seeing me again when you were still officially married to your first husband Curtis (even though, technically, you weren't even living in the same house, but still); considering your mom doesn't really owe you a wedding under the circumstances, but is giving you one anyway, so you might just want to watch it every once in a while and not push your luck.

My band was nervous about the wedding too. Three of them came up from California—Nate on bass, Carlos on drums, Fischer on guitar and lead vocals, which I used to do and he used to back me up, but now that I'm gone it's his deal—and I told them to go ahead and play good stuff but don't get too crazy. Because we have plenty of songs that are great, if I do say so, but that aren't totally frightening to fifty-year-old Mormon people. So Carlos was like, "Jimmy, what if they boo us off the stage? What if they get all offended and leave right in the middle?" And I said, "Don't worry, most of them are pretty cool, that I've met. Also they have some halfway decent radio stations in Salt Lake, surprise surprise, and somebody's got to be listening to them, right? It's not like they've never heard our kind of music before."

And wouldn't you know it, people actually danced? It took a while, though. At first it was just me and Tina; then I started dancing with her little girl Ava, who's six years old and the greatest kid ever. She was wearing this dress she picked out herself that was all lacy and poufy and pink—a dress Tina just hated, but Ava loved it so she let her have it—and she kept saying, "Twirl me like a princess, Jimmy." Understand that I don't exactly know how to twirl anybody like a princess, so I just scooped her up and spun her around in my arms. I must have done something right, because she was smiling and laughing, having the time of her life. Then Marnie came out dancing with her oldest boy, who I forget his name because she has three of them and they're hard to keep straight, but that seemed to loosen everybody up. Before you knew it a whole bunch of Mormons were out on the dance floor, having a great time. Even Mr. and Mrs. Palmer were dancing—kind of timid, tap-your-toes around dancing—but dancing, still. It counted. And you should have seen Tina smiling. So happy. My dad came up while we were dancing a slow song and whispered in my ear, "So can I have a turn with this beautiful girl?" And I said, "Be my guest." It was really cool watching both of them dance, because they're the two people I love most in the world.

Even just a couple years ago, I wouldn't have believed a scene like that could ever come true. Tina had taken off back in '94 and I figured it was for good. I figured I deserved it. I still have this picture in my mind of the morning she left: Tina standing at the front door of the house we shared with the guys in the band, her backpack on her shoulder, her mouth a hard line. "I'm outta here," she said. At the time I didn't believe her. I was too wasted, thought everything was a joke. I said, "Baby, come on, come back. I'll stop it. I promise." The drugs, the craziness. Everything. But I didn't mean it. She

171

could tell I didn't mean it. "Liar," she called me. Then she said, "You better not come looking for me till you get your head straight. I'm not kidding," and she walked out the door and out of my life. Once I figured out for sure she was gone, I wanted to get in my car and chase after her, head to Utah and look up her parents in the phone book and find her and make her take me back. But I knew Tina. When she says a thing she means it. And what would my story be with her parents, anyway? Nice, clean-cut types—I'd seen pictures, heard stories—and they're supposed to be okay with their daughter hooking up with some drugged-up musician with no job? Don't think so. So I gave up on her, let time go by. It took me a while, still, to get clean. A few more personal disasters and finally I came to my senses. "What the hell am I doing?" I asked myself. "What's the point, even, of living?" That's when my dad stepped up and got me into a drug program, and I came out of it a new person. Better. And my first thought, after that, was Tina.

When I took off to go find her last year, my friends said I was crazy. Insane. "It's been six years, Jimmy," they said. "Six years and not even a hello. She's probably married and fat with a couple of kids and some vague fuzzy memory of you and that's it." But then, they didn't want me to leave them or the band. Even if I hadn't been chasing after Tina, though, I would have left the band anyway. I never told them that. But the lifestyle wasn't right for me anymore. As strong as I thought I was, who knows what can happen to a person when he's constantly in that environment? Besides, I was twenty-six years old, and still we were mostly playing in bars around town waiting for the big payday, the same old story you hear from bands all over L.A., and I'd had enough. Time to move on, grow up, be a man. Time to settle down. And Tina was the only person I'd ever met in my life I wanted to settle down with.

Finding her was easier than I thought it would be. I did what I'd wished I could do back in '94: drove up to Salt Lake and got myself a room at a Holiday Inn, found her parents' number in the phone book—Nathan Palmer, the only one in there, lucky for me—took a deep breath, and called it. And guess who answered the phone? Tina. Just one word, Hello, and I knew it was her. My heart started beating all out of control, and I almost hung the phone up because who would have expected *she* would be the one to answer, but I told myself, *Courage, man, be brave.* So I go, "Tina?" And immediately, like we'd been talking on the phone all the time these last few years, she says, "Jimmy?" And I say, "Yeah, hey, how's it going?" And she says, "Jimmy Moretti, for real?" Then I can tell in her voice she's happy to hear from me, which makes everything worth it. The rehab, leaving the band behind, the crazy drive to Utah with a couple hundred bucks in my pocket and no job and no plans, no nothing but the thought of hearing her voice and having it sound just like it did. Surprised, but glad.

At that moment I didn't even think about complications. I didn't think, *Hey, wonder why she's living with her parents when she's twenty-six years old, and what about that kid's voice I hear in the background?* I was just so glad I found her that I rushed right up to her house. Now I'd be lying if I said I wasn't nervous to see her again, because you never know how a person can change after all that time, but when she opened the door to let me in, I could hardly believe my luck. Better looking, even, than before. And that smile! Just the same. She threw her arms around me and said, "Jimmy, I wondered if you'd ever straighten yourself out and come up here and claim me," and I thought, *That's my girl. As bold as ever.* Except she wasn't mine to claim. Not then, anyway. She told me straight out about Curtis and how she'd left him but that they weren't quite divorced. My first question was, "Did he hurt you? Did he damage you in any way?" And she says, "No, no, he's a good guy; I'm the one who did the hurting." So I say, "How?" And she says, "Jimmy, I'm not always the person I want to be. Sometimes I hurt the people I'm supposed to love, and I need to warn you about that." Then I ask her, "Do you still love him?" And she says, "That's the problem. I never loved him like I should—like a wife's supposed to love her husband—and I just couldn't keep on lying anymore."

The next couple months were pretty tricky. I got myself a job at a warehouse driving a forklift—not too bad, $11.50 an hour and good overtime—and I found a little apartment and pretty soon Tina wanted to move in with me, but her parents weren't too happy about the idea. Which I totally got, since the divorce wasn't even official, plus her parents don't approve of people living together before marriage —even though we already had, back in California. They kept saying to Tina, "What about Ava?" And they were right. She was confused already about the divorce, living with her mom at her grandma and grandpa's house sometimes, and at her dad's house other times. So I told Tina that I didn't want to get off on the wrong foot with her family. I could understand their suspicions. I mean, who was I to them? Some guitarist? Some stranger? And after being with her again for only a couple of months, I knew I wanted to be with her all the time. Marry her. So I said, "Be patient. We've got to do this right."

The whole thing's been hard on Curtis. He's been purposefully avoiding me, but we can't help running into each other now that Ava's in my life, too. When we do meet up, he doesn't say much to me. In fact, he hardly even looks my way. But at least he hasn't tried to beat my head in, which he could do, if he wanted to. I feel for the guy, though. Tina's a hard one to shake. I know I never could.

And now I don't have to. We have our wedding pictures collected in a big brown leather book and I like to flip through them sometimes. Take a look at how my life has changed this past year. There's Tina, so beautiful in her silky white dress; Tina's big, smiley family—people who totally don't get me yet, but are still grinning for the camera, willing to try to make it work; cute little Ava, my step-daughter now—step-daughter!— which I still can't believe; and of course my dad, and the guys from the band, happy for me even though I left them over some crazy idea that I could head up to Utah, of all places, and start myself a life.

After we'd been married about a week or so Tina asked me, "Jimmy, are you happy?" And I was truthful when I told her, "Yes, I am happy. Happy as I've ever been." Then she said, "You've got to promise me one thing. You tell me if you're ever unhappy, because it'll kill a marriage quicker than anything, pretending to be happy when you're not." I told her, "I promise. But I can't foresee that particular turn of events, anyhow, so don't you worry." She kissed me then, and held on to me tight, and whispered in my ear, "Pray it won't. Pray it won't." Then I said, "Hey, you," and took her face in my hands so I could look her right in the eye. "This time it's going to work," I said. And she smiled, huge, beautiful. Believing me.

Alicia—2006

&

FAITHFUL

My daughter Beth sits at the kitchen table staring down at her breakfast. I tell her to eat. Eat! She looks brittle and pale, as if her system doesn't have the energy to pump blood from one end of her body to the other. "You're getting too thin," I say, and she shakes her head. I ask her, "Do you want something else? Cereal? Toast? Anything."

Finally she speaks. "No," she whispers. "No, I'm fine."

I made her scrambled eggs and bacon. Hearty foods. I gesture at her plate. "If you eat this you'll feel better." Her eyes are so empty. Food, at least, I can fill her with, and yet she won't let me.

"I want to call Kyle."

I think her body has forgotten how to be hungry. If she doesn't eat now, I'm afraid she never will, not all day long, not tomorrow. Without me here to watch her, maybe she'll never eat again and allow herself to disappear.

"I have to call him," she says. "I'm going to."

I pierce a bit of egg with my fork and hold it to her. "Open your mouth," I say. "Eat this."

"Mom," she tells me. "Enough."

Yesterday, I was the one who answered the phone when Kyle's mother called to tell us he'd been hospitalized. She's a bitter woman who delights in bad news. "He doesn't want to see you. None of you," she said, and her voice was full of triumph. My first thought was that Kyle had attempted suicide. He's never tried it before, but I've read all the literature about bipolar disorder. It's a serious risk and I've been worried about it for months. But no. "He checked himself in," she told me. "He was afraid he'd do himself harm, and he wanted to get somewhere safe before he did. He's been all alone. You people left him all alone."

You people. I wanted to argue with her but didn't know what to say.

After Beth calls the hospital she comes to me and says they're letting him out.

"How soon?" I ask.

"Three days."

"Three days? How can he be ready to go in three days? How can they do that?"

"It's what they do. It's how they do things." She sighs. The skin around her eyes is swollen from crying. "He won't live with his mother. He can't be alone."

I lean my forehead against my palms.

"He has nowhere to go," she says.

I look at her: my daughter, so young and so old. I can see her spirit shriveling up inside her, curling in on itself like a fallen leaf. I don't know if I can ever forgive him.

"Please," she says. "We have to. He's my husband."

Beth goes with her father to the hospital but I decide to stay back. "Somebody needs to be here with Stella," I tell them, because after all a psychiatric hospital is no place for a baby. While they're gone, I finish making up my daughter Marnie's old room for Kyle. I fan out a selection of magazines on the nightstand; I fold a stack of towels in the closet; I dust off the blinds and turn them so the light can come in. Light is important, I know. The worst thing people can do when they're depressed is block out the sun.

I hear Stella's voice coming from Beth's room to let me know she's up from her nap. She's the only baby I've ever known who doesn't wake up crying. She wakes up pleasant, babbling her cheerful baby language, happy to wait to be rescued from her crib. I open the door and see she's pulled herself up to stand. She gives me her wide, gummy smile and opens and closes her fist in a gesture of hello. Her grandpa taught her how.

"Hello, Smiley," I say.

She bounces up and down in her crib. Stella is a beautiful child, delightful and easy. She deserves every happiness.

"Daddy's coming," I tell her. "Let's get you ready."

I dress her in a little yellow jumper and sweep her hair to the top of her head and tie it with a ribbon. She's not quite one, but already she's learning her words, like "ball" and "up." She calls Nathan "Papa," short for Grandpa. He seems to be Stella's favorite person, and I don't know what Nathan will do when she and Beth are gone. They've only been living here a little over six months, and already it seems like they've always been with us.

Stella won't know her father. In the four months since Thanksgiving, Kyle has seen his daughter only twice. Both visits with her were awkward and quick, hardly memorable enough to make an impression on a baby. And who knows what state he'll be in now? There's a chance he won't want to interact with her, or with any one of us.

I was surprised he agreed to live here after the difficulties of the last few months. He's been furious at the whole family and with me in particular, holding us responsible for keeping Beth from him and ruining his life. Although we haven't seen him much, he's been in touch, sending all of us rambling and vitriolic letters that detail our

179

many faults and sins against him. He even mailed a couple off to Marnie and Mike in Minnesota, calling Marnie weak-willed and Mike an "arrogant S.O.B. living leechlike off the flesh of the poor." Neither of them were too offended by the letters—after all, they're intelligent people; they understand mental illness and that the real Kyle, the Kyle they used to know, would never have said such things. But in those letters I saw Kyle spiraling even further out of control. I finally used the word I've avoided saying to Beth all this time: Divorce. "Walk away," I told her. "Start again. You're still young and beautiful, and there are plenty of good men who'd be thrilled to have you." She went so far as to contact an attorney, but on the day of the appointment, she backed out. She called me from the bank where she works as a teller and let me know.

"I can't do it," she said. "It isn't right. He's sick! If he had cancer or had an accident and was paralyzed, would you tell me to walk away from him then too?"

"But he's not taking his medicine. He's not trying. He can't be a husband to you or a father to Stella in such a state. He's dangerous and unpredictable, and I'm not going to let him ruin your life."

"He's not dangerous," she shot back. "He's never hurt me. He's never hurt anybody."

"Maybe not physically."

"It's not his fault."

I paused. This is where I find myself struggling. I am sympathetic to depression. I understand. I know that mental illness is biological and often genetic, a disease. But people can *choose* to fight it. I know they can. They can choose to take their medications and go to their therapy sessions and do everything in their power to keep back the demons. Kyle has not demonstrated a willingness to do this.

"Beth." I sighed. "Honey."

"This is not your life, Mom. It's mine," she said, then hung up the phone.

And now he's coming here. To live with us. I plant Stella on my hip and head downstairs. We have a routine, Stella and I: breakfast, playtime, naptime, lunch, more playtime, naptime, and then either Beth or Nathan comes home. Beth is enrolled full-time in dental hygiene school and works twenty hours a week at the bank. We want her to make the most of her opportunities while she's with us, prepare herself for the possibility of a life as a single mother. I don't mind staying home with Stella. I thought I would—heaven knows my memories of mothering little children aren't the fondest—but things are different this time. I'm older, wiser, more patient. And it's much easier to take care of a child when you know that, ultimately, the responsibility for raising her falls to someone else.

I strap Stella in her high chair and mix up a bowl of rice cereal and applesauce. I sit down to feed her and immediately hear the garage door rising. My body stiffens—my heart runs quick—and I take a couple of long deep breaths to steady myself. I already know what I will do: look him in the eye, smile pleasantly, say, "Hello, Kyle, good to see you," and leave it at that. Short. Sweet. The last time he saw me, he was furious and wanted to argue, to bait me, accusing me of shallow-heartedness (that was the term he used— shallow-hearted—original, descriptive, reminding me of all the things I used to like about him), and I am ashamed to say that he got the better of me and I fought right back, forcing Beth to stand between us as a kind of mute referee while we hurled our accusations across the room at each other. But I've steeled my will this time. I won't give in. No matter what he says, I refuse to fight in front of his daughter. Or mine.

"We're home," Beth calls, coming in from the garage. My back is to them while I spoon cereal into Stella's mouth. I can't bear, yet, to turn around. I hear feet shuffling, the thump of luggage being stacked inside the door.

"I think somebody's excited to see his daughter," Nathan says.

So I turn around. There he is: Kyle. Pale, puffy, heavy-lidded. His hair is cut shorter than I remember it being—too short, a sloppy buzz cut—and it makes his head look unwieldy and disproportionate, wobbling slightly atop his shoulders. He was so handsome once. A

181

beautiful boy, smooth-skinned and strong, so vibrant that life seemed to emanate from him in waves, like light, like heat. Now here he stands ravaged. Undone. I prepare myself for whatever he has to say to me.

"Alicia," he says. "I'm sorry. I'm sorry." He begins to sob, his shoulders shaking, his chest heaving. He drops the duffel bag he's holding, then comes to me with his arms outstretched and wraps them around me. I feel lost inside them, swallowed up. I touch my hand to his back and pat it lightly. "It's okay," I whisper. "Kyle, stop crying; it's okay. We're okay."

He raises his head from where he has buried it in my shoulder and looks at me, his face just inches from mine, and I am frightened by the despair in his eyes. The ragged sorrow. "I never meant . . ." he begins, his voice tremulous. "I want to try . . ."

I step back slowly, gently, disentangling myself from his embrace.

"Don't worry, now," I say. "See Stella? She's been waiting for you."

Beth has Stella in her arms. She comes toward him. Kyle continues to cry, the tears running freely down his cheeks. "She's so beautiful." He reaches out and touches her face. "The most beautiful girl."

Nathan puts a hand on Kyle's shoulder. "How about we head upstairs? It's been quite a day. You should sleep, get some of your strength back. Okay? That sound okay?"

Kyle nods and lets Nathan lead him up to his room. Beth stands at the foot of the stairs, her back curved just slightly from the weight of Stella in her arms, watching them go.

For the next two days Kyle stays in bed, venturing out only to go to the bathroom. Mostly Beth takes care of him, getting him food and books, dragging the little television from the basement up the stairs and balancing it on top of the dresser so Kyle has a way to pass the time. Tomorrow she goes back to work and school, and so does Nathan. I'll be alone in the house with Stella and Kyle.

"Don't worry, Mom," Beth tells me. We're sitting on the family room floor folding laundry together, a load of whites. Beth has marked all her garments with a tiny "B" on the tag, so I can tell hers from mine. "I can see a difference in him already. The medication's working. He's evening out."

"He'll take the medication himself, right? You don't have to force him?"

"He's taking it. He promises me this time he'll take it no fail, no matter what. I believe him too."

"I'm glad you believe him." I take one of Stella's tiny under-shirts and fold it carefully, first lengthwise, then in half. I don't look up from my work. "It's good to be hopeful."

"Please, Mom, just do me a favor."

I lift my head. Beth's gaze is steady. Implacable. She knows what I'm saying. That I don't trust him.

" Give him an inch," she says. "One little inch."

What do you think I'm doing? I feel like saying. *He's living in my home! I'm washing his clothes! What do all of you expect from me?*

"I'll make sure he's taken care of, Beth," I say. I fold a pair of Kyle's socks, put them in Beth's basket.

"He can get better." Her face is drawn and thin but fierce, sharp with the strain of longing. "He's doing it this time. He's trying. He checked himself in, didn't he? Voluntarily. This time is different. We need to have faith."

We need to have faith. Yes. But faith in what? Faith that God will change our lives and make them easier? Or is the more difficult faith required of us, the kind that says no matter the load we're asked to carry, for the love of God we will do our duty and endure? I fear it is the latter.

"I understand about faith," I tell her. "I know."

Monday afternoon, Stella is asleep and I am in the kitchen mak-ing rolls. The air smells fresh and yeasty, and the yellow sunlight of almost-spring spilling in through the windows is warm against my skin. I punch down the risen dough, my hands white with flour, and roll it out flat. The silence, the light around me, the smell of sustenance, all of it relaxes me, so when I see Kyle coming down the stairs I am able to be pleasant and calm, as if he's a houseguest who's staying with us for a short, friendly visit.

"Hello there," I say. "You feeling better?"

His smile is quick and glad. He seems surprised at my easiness. "Yes," he says. "A little. A little better every day."

"Good." The dough sticks between my fingers. "Good news."

He comes up beside me in his pajamas and socks, breathing loudly, nervous. "Can I help you? Do something? Old time's sake, you know."

Once, Kyle had been my cooking assistant, my trainee. My daughters weren't much interested in the kitchen, but Kyle was always comfortable here. As the only child of a single mother, cooking was a skill he'd taught himself. I remember him telling me how he experimented with recipes as a kid, trying to make something tasty from the odd bits and ends of ingredients he could find in his almost-empty cupboards. That piece of his history tied him to me. I did the same thing when I was young, making mother-food for myself, lacking a mother who would do it for me. When he and Beth started dating, it was Kyle who joined me in the kitchen on Sundays. I taught him how to make soups and stews, apple pies, marinades for every kind of meat. Some Sundays, if I was late coming home from church, I'd be greeted by the smell of dinner already under way and find Kyle in the kitchen, grinning, the counter covered with opened cans and spice jars and dirty bowls. He was always an impulsive cook, often working without a recipe, messy and scattershot. I was never able to change that about him. But his meals seemed to turn out every time, I must say, sometimes even better than mine.

"I'm almost done here," I say. I brush my hands together and flour hangs in the air for a moment, like a cloud.

"I could roll them up," he says. "I can't ruin that, can I?"

I haven't even cut them into triangles yet, and already Kyle can tell I'm making crescent rolls. He's helped me enough. He knows.

"Then, sure," I say. "That would be fine."

I allow myself to work in the silence between us, me rolling out and cutting the dough, Kyle wrapping up the pastries into delicate spirals and placing them on the metal sheet. We work quickly together, still. His fingers are fast. I slide the rolls inside the oven. "Thank you," I say. "Many hands make light work."

"I know. Which is why I'm here."

For a moment my anger flashes. Is he trying to tell me that he thinks he's here to help *me*, somehow? Is he still that deluded? But then I look into his plaintive face and understand his meaning. He means to say he's here because he needs all our hands, every hand in the family, if he has any hope of getting well.

"I've made life very difficult. For Beth. For you. For all of you." He sounds quiet but steady, the steadiest I've heard him in months. "I can see why you'd want me out, away, gone. If Beth was my daughter . . ." His voice trails away.

"I love her, is all. I don't want to see her hurt."

"I'm afraid she's hurt already. I'm afraid, no matter what happens now—I go, I stay, I die, I live—she's hurt. I've been trying to figure out a way around it, but there is none."

I sigh. Smart boy. "Yes," I say. "True."

"So what do you want me to do?" He spreads his arms out wide, imploring me. His face is worried and small. "Tell me. Anything. Whatever you tell me to do I will do it."

I remember back almost three years ago when we first got the diagnosis. We were all desperate and scared, but ready to fight, ready to win. The first time he went off his meds and relapsed, we rallied around him. "You can do it, Kyle. We're here. Be strong!" And he was, for a time. He seemed so much like his old self that when Beth became pregnant I even allowed myself to be optimistic. But then Stella came and Kyle's crash was so swift, so terrible. I can't get the sight of my daughter out of my head: Beth holding her newborn in her arms and sobbing from fear and exhaustion and confusion and betrayal, her young body limp and drained of hope. I vowed then I would never trust him again. Never again.

"You just do what you need to do, Kyle. Get better. Do your best."

Stella's voice floats down the stairs. She is up from her nap.

"I'd better go get her." I start up the stairs, but then I feel his hand on my wrist, stopping me. I turn and look down at him.

"What," I say.

"Do you still love me?" he whispers. His voice is very small. He is so young, still, not quite twenty-five. A boy. He doesn't look me in the face but at a point just past my shoulder. "You did, before. I know you did."

"Kyle, I . . ." My voice trails away. I hear Stella, rattling against the bars of her crib.

He finds my face, looks at me straight. "It's a yes or no question. Please just answer it."

I close my eyes and try to find the Kyle I loved. My almost-son. It is easy: in my memory he has taken up residence in corners and rooms and he is lodged there, permanent, his place as sure as if he had been born to it. This boy not of my flesh, not of my blood, but grafted in.

"You know I do," I answer. Then I go and get his child.

A couple of weeks into Kyle's stay with us, Beth asks if the two of them can move into the master bedroom. Be together. It is not an unprecedented request. The only queen-size bed in the house is our bed, the bed Nathan built for my birthday so long ago. Whenever married couples come and stay, Nathan and I vacate it and sleep singly in one of the girls' rooms. But I am surprised.

"Are you sure?" I ask her. "Is this what you want?"

She is still pale, still drawn, still much too thin. She nods.

"You know what this will mean to him," I say. "That you're coming back. That you're recommitted."

186

She nods again.

"So you're sure?"

She pulls in a deep breath and holds it. "I've given up on being sure. Is that a terrible thing to admit?"

I circle my arm around her thin shoulders. "Not terrible," I say. "Brave."

She looks up at me. Her eyes are teary, but the lift of her head speaks strength to me, and determination. "I haven't been able to imagine my life without him. I tried to. But I can't."

I rub her arm, and her skin is cold beneath my fingers.

"Can you understand?" she asks.

"You love him," I say. "Of course I understand."

Later that week I wake up in the night thirsty. I slide out of bed and creep into the hall, careful not to wake the baby, and when I pass Kyle and Beth's room I see the door is pushed slightly ajar. They are curled in toward each other, sleeping, their heads almost touching and Beth's arm slung loosely across Kyle's side. Seeing them reminds me how difficult it is for two bodies, even sleeping, to face each other and not turn away. I close the door gently, and leave them to themselves.

Tess—2007

෪

BOUND ON EARTH

The restaurant pulsates with noise. Francesco's is a family place —ideal for a party—but the older she gets, the more Tess struggles to hold a conversation in such a setting. The family reserved a party room, tucked around a corner and partially out of sight, but it's impossible to escape the clamor of a restaurant during the Saturday night rush. And Saturday rush or no, the growing Palmer family can create a ruckus all its own.

Tess's granddaughter, Beth, sits across the table, her hair long and loose and a shade lighter than Tess remembers. Perhaps she's been to a salon recently. That would be a good sign, wouldn't it?

"You look lovely, my dear," Tess says, her voice raised a notch.

"What?" Beth asks. She isn't looking at Tess. She's trying to distract her little girl, Stella, feeding her breadsticks one bit at a time.

"You look lovely. Your hair." Louder still.

Beth tucks a stray lock behind her ear. "Oh!" She smiles, just a little. "Thanks."

The din of this place is nearly overwhelming. Laughter, the clank of silverware and dishes, the electronic buzzer on the front door going off every time a person enters or leaves, not to mention the "old-fashioned" juke-box in the corner (the children are fascinated and keep begging for quarters). But it's a noisy, noisy world, Tess reminds herself. So many lives being lived.

Tess reaches her hand across the table and lays it atop her grand-daughter's. She needs to connect. It's been weeks since she's seen Beth. Who knows how long it will be until they get another chance to talk?

Beth's hand is small and warm beneath her own, and the touch of her skin reminds Tess how much she misses holding hands. It's been twenty-five years, now, since Joel's death. Twenty-five years since she's held anyone's hand but that of a very young child. Other than the occasional embrace or a simple pat on a knee, Tess keeps her hands to herself. In the last few years, her hands have become alien to her, almost startling: the thick, ropy veins; the twisted knuckles; the age spots splattered like drops of dried paint. She often keeps them clasped and curled in her lap so she won't have to look at them and be reminded that she's not as young as she thinks she is. That yes, death is approaching.

And it is approaching. Approaching much too quickly. When the doctor told her the news it took her breath away. Six months. "That's a snap of my fingers," she told him. "A blink of an eye." He didn't disagree.

"How are you?" Tess asks her granddaughter. She tries to hold her gaze.

"Oh, good! Fine." Beth flashes Tess a quick smile and then pulls her hand away. Stella is arching her back in her high chair, hollering to be set free, and Beth unlatches the chair's safety strap and lifts her daughter out in one swift, practiced move. "Kyle?" Beth says loudly, trying to draw her husband's attention from across the table. "Could you follow her? Make sure she doesn't wander out of here?" But already Stella has made a beeline for the restaurant's front doors. Kyle jumps up from his chair and sprints after her.

Kyle's looking better, Tess can see. In the months since his hospitalization he's lost a little weight, regained a touch color in his cheeks. He can still be mercurial and moody—but he will *always* be, she's got to remember. When Kyle was a teenager Tess had pegged him as a passionate soul, but back then it was more endearing than alarming. Now, the family celebrates the progress he makes, but it's coupled with an undercurrent of wary watchfulness. Since he and Beth moved into their own place a couple of months ago, the whole family has been on symptom-alert. Which is why, Tess realizes, Beth pulled her hand away so quickly. Being the subject of constant scrutiny and sympathy can be utterly exhausting. Tess remembers. It's much easier to behave as if life is normal and hope everyone else plays along. So she will respect her granddaughter's needs and leave her be.

Yes, it can be a relief to be an old woman, allowed to sit in a corner, silent, and observe. She loves listening to the boisterous conversation of the grandchildren—adults now, all of them, in their twenties and thirties but still so young—without being expected to participate. Over the years, solitude has become an unexpected friend. A comfort. When Joel died, Tess was only fifty-six years old, and the specter of decades of silence and isolation had frightened her deeply at the time. She'd never been alone in her life. Not even for a night. Always there had been parents, brothers, sisters, her husband, her children. After Joel's death, it took her months to fall asleep alone in her bed without the radio. She kept it on all night, the music humming softly, even entering her dreams. But after a few months, she started to make peace with her solitude. After a few years, she came to like it. When grandchildren visited, she reveled in their laughter and chattering and running. But when she shut the door at the end of the night and the quiet settled around her, as soothing as a well-worn blanket, she was glad.

But Tess still enjoys days like today. It's Alicia and Nathan's thirty-fifth wedding anniversary, and everyone has gathered to celebrate. All Tess's children are here: Nathan, obviously, but also Christy and Russell and their spouses. Even one of Alicia's step-brothers has made an appearance, along with his wife. And all the kids are in town. Marnie and Mike have flown in from Minnesota with their four boys—oh, the plane ride, what a headache that must have been! —but they've come, and Alicia and Nathan are thrilled.

"Grandma T!" It's Tina, coming in with Jimmy and Ava and little Zadie. Tess hadn't been sure about that name—Sadie, maybe, but Zadie? Whoever heard of such a thing?—but the kids have taken to calling her "Zee" and it seems to suit her. She's a firecracker, with a thick shock of black hair and mischievous blue eyes. She'll give those two a run for their money.

"Hello there, dear. Hello Jimmy." Tess opens her arms wide and Ava runs into them, then kisses her sloppily on the cheek.

Tina leans in for a hug. "How you feeling?"

"Oh, fine. Fine. As good as ever."

"Indestructible Grandma, that's what I call you. We just came back from visiting Jimmy's grandma and she can't even walk down the hall without help, I swear! I was going to tell her how you still volunteer at the hospital and vacuum like a maniac, but Jimmy didn't want me to make her feel bad."

"Well, she *is* my grandma," Jimmy says. "Don't want her to think we're having grandma competitions."

Tina grins. "Well Grandma T would win hands down. You'll end up one of those they spotlight on *The Today Show*, 'One hundred and four years old and still bottling her own jam' and all that."

Tess smiles weakly. For the first time since she heard the news last week, she feels like a liar. She's rationalized her silence thus far, especially with the anniversary celebration to consider. Nothing ruins a party like a dying grandma! But when she's honest with herself, she realizes she doesn't want to tell anyone at all. Not now. Not ever. She wants to go on as she is, loved but also blithely ignored. And cancer can be such a difficult disease. So hard on the family. After working as a nurse for twenty-seven years, Tess understands this better than most. For years, she prayed she might dodge this particular diagnosis and die peacefully in her sleep. She actually felt a twinge of envy when she heard about the passing of a church general authority's wife who died while sitting next to her husband on the couch, watching television. One moment here, the next moment gone, and no medicines and doctors and treatments and traumas left in her wake. What a blessing!

"Everybody's finally shown up, so it's time for the big to-do," Marnie says. She stands at the front of the room, eyebrows raised, hands on her hips. Always the show-runner, that girl. Tess sees Tina look over at Jimmy and roll her eyes in response to the subtle dig at her tardiness.

Marnie's oldest boys come to the front of the room holding a poster board covered with pictures: Alicia and Nathan as tow-headed kids; Alicia and Nathan and the whole Palmer clan at their wedding thirty-five years ago (and one look at the scandalously short cut of Tess's own skirt shows that yes, it was the early seventies, and even Mothers of the Groom were influenced by fashion); Alicia and Nathan in their thirties, tan and healthy and so beautiful, both of them; Alicia and Nathan waving from the deck of a cruise ship, just last year.

Tess has found it a pleasure to watch their relationship grow and solidify. When they married, Tess must admit, she wasn't sure. Alicia's strong personality could dominate Nathan's, especially early on. Tess remembers literally biting her own tongue at times, the only way to keep herself from leaping to her son's defense. Once, at a family get-together, Alicia made a comment about the financial strain of living as a schoolteacher's wife that pushed Tess past the boiling point. She pulled Nathan aside and said, "Stick up for yourself, son!" but Nathan's expression hardened into a grimace. "We're figuring it out, Mom," he said. "And like you should talk." Coming from Nathan those were fighting words, and she never meddled in his marriage again.

Marnie points to the poster and gives an accounting (as she knows it) of her parents' life together. She tells funny stories, mostly, anecdotes everyone knows, and the people in this room who love Alicia and Nathan—who can't imagine a world without them in it together, as a couple—smile and sigh and nod. When the laughing dies down, Marnie talks as eloquently as she can over the restaurant's clatter, saying things about love and fidelity and example and companionship. She mentions her father's sweetness, and her voice catches. "We saw the way he looked at you, Mom, and there was never any doubt about how he felt. Never any doubt that he loved you."

Tess glances over at Marie's husband Mike. His head is turned—he's shushing one of the boys—and it's obvious he hasn't heard her. *Mike!* Tess wants to tell him. *Turn around. Listen to your wife!* Mike's a good man. A good provider. But so busy, and gone all the time. Tess worries that Marnie is lonely. Sometimes, there's a dimness in her eyes Tess recognizes. Remembers.

"Now the grandkids are going to sing a song," Marnie says.

All seven of them shamble up to the front, baby Zee on Ava's hip, and Marnie's youngest, Jonathan, threatening to toddle away. Even though Beth's Stella isn't even two, she grabs Ava's free hand and stands still and straight. She's practiced this moment.

Marnie starts the CD player, and a familiar tinkly piano introduction begins. It's "Close to You," by the Carpenters, that sentimental love song from the '70s. It must have been Nathan and Alicia's song. Tess didn't know. But she can tell from the tears in Alicia's eyes that it must have been.

The children's voices are high and thin and sweetly off-key. By the second verse, they've fallen hopelessly behind the music. Marnie crouches down in front of them, mouthing the words, waving her arms, but they are oblivious and soldier on, a smattering of childish warbles mixing with the *"Ahhh, ahhhhh, close to you,"* of the canned backup singers on the taped accompaniment. Even though they are supposed to be in a private room, it's obvious the patrons in the main dining area can hear them. They're craning their necks, trying to peek in. A waitress has stopped near their table, her tray loaded with dishes, her head cocked to the side and a wistful smile on her face.

Stars falling from the sky, birds appearing, angels sprinkling moon dust. The words of love songs. Tess looks around at her children and grandchildren, their spouses, considering these marriages as they really are. No birds. No angels. Has this been a disappointment to them? Were they expecting golden starlight, believing it was their due?

The children finish and everyone claps. Tess calls out, "Bravo, bravo!"

Then Marnie turns and looks at her. "Grandma, I know this is out of the blue, but we were wondering if you'd like to say anything. You've known Mom and Dad longer than any of us. Any memories? Any advice?"

Tess's stomach somersaults. This is a surprise. And what to say? Before she can speak, her eyes suddenly fill with tears. What if this is the last time she sees them all together? What can she tell them that they'll remember? She takes a deep breath, steadies herself and stands.

"Well, now," she begins. "I knew your Dad had found somebody special the minute he started telling me about Alicia. I could see it on his face. He looked so, I don't know. Pleased with himself."

Alicia shakes her head, smiling and embarrassed. But it was true—Nathan loved showing her off, taking her places. Joel was still alive then, but sick, and Nathan was so anxious for him to meet her and offer his silent approval. Tess remembers Alicia perched on the edge of their living room couch, leaning toward Joel just slightly, her eyes fixed on his. So interested. She hung on every word he said, no matter how long it took him to say it. Joel never frightened her, and he loved her for it. When he died, Alicia cried harder than Christy did.

"But I should say something about marriage. Something wise." She smiles and her family laughs approvingly. It's so easy to get a laugh when you're eighty-one. She pauses. What should she tell them? Her own marriage—happy, then tragic, then strained, then, strangely, peaceful—it wasn't a typical marriage, no. But whose is?

"When I married your grandfather in the temple, I was bound

195

to him forever. I don't think I quite understood what that meant at the time. We were both very young. And very attractive." Another laugh. "Most of you didn't know your grandfather. He was a good man, a good father, and he got sick. Nathan remembers."

Nathan nods, barely perceptible. He was a teenager when Joel had his stroke, a middle child and the eldest of Tess's two boys. Joel changed from a charming, jovial father to a quiet, sometimes bitter old man in a matter of months. Tess watched Nathan turning inward right along with him. She couldn't do anything about it.

"It was hard," she says, and looks down at her hands. Soon, these veins will be punctured by IV needles. There will be tubes and tape. And soon after that, her hands will be still. Someone will slip her wedding ring from her finger and give it to her daughter as a remembrance. Then her hands will be folded one final time and placed in her lap. "I chose your grandfather long before I had any idea what marriage was all about." She stops. Sighs. This is sounding like a lecture. The room is growing still, the easy laughter silenced. Grandma doesn't talk like this, so openly. Even the little children are quiet. "But you get married and you work hard and you try; then you look around and suddenly there's a room like this, full of all these people you love. It's amazing, really. A miracle."

She looks into the faces of her family—these people who trust her, people who love her, people who will gladly take care of her—and she still can't imagine telling them she's going to die. How would she feel if one of them was sick and didn't reach out? Hurt, of course, and confused, and maybe even a little bit angry. She can't tell herself that she's keeping the cancer a secret for the sake of her family. No. It's her own fear. Her own pride. How can it be that she's lived this long and the same demons still beset her?

"None of us is perfect," Tess says, "which is a wonderful thing. The scriptures tell us that God gives us weaknesses because he loves us. So that we can turn to him. So that we can turn to each other. Only then can we be strong."

Now she is starting to cry. Today is not the day to tell them. But tomorrow, she will. She will pick up the phone and call them all and tell them she needs their help. She will give them that gift before she goes.

"But enough from me. Enough!" She waves her hand in front of her face. "I'm an old woman and I'm sentimental."

She notices Alicia has moved in beside her, and her daughter-in-law pats her gently on the shoulder. Everyone is silent for two beats, for three.

"Thank you, Tess. So much. That was lovely," Alicia says. "Now how about dessert?"

Tess smiles up at Alicia, grateful for the rescue. She takes a moment and dabs at her eyes.

Ever frugal, Alicia has brought dessert from home. The children swarm around her, begging for two scoops of ice cream and the biggest slice of cake, and just like that, the attention in the room shifts. Wives turn to husbands, fathers to children, and life keeps spinning forward, loose and free as a ribbon off a spool. Tess stays in her chair. Any minute now a grandchild will bring her a plate, and she won't beg off and request just a sliver, as she has for years and years. She'll take the thick slice they offer her and enjoy every bite.

She closes her eyes and listens to their voices. Her family. Hers. And Joel's too. She imagines his presence close by, listening right alongside her. How anxious he must be to see her again. Does it hurt his feelings that she doesn't want to leave quite yet? She speaks to him in her mind, the same way she has done since the day he died: *Don't worry, my dear. I'm still all yours.*

It is hard to imagine eternity. The vastness of it. The emptiness waiting to be filled. She trusts there will be children there, and music, and cake, and husbands and wives and daughters and sons. It will be heaven, after all. And she is not afraid.

Angela Hallstrom lives in South Jordan, Utah, with her husband and four children. Her fiction has received awards from the Utah Arts Council and has appeared or is forthcoming in *Dialogue*, the *New Era*, *Irreantum*, and *Salt Flats Annual*. She holds an MFA in creative writing from Hamline University and teaches writing at Salt Lake Community College.

Printed in the United States
105557LV00005B/68/P